ALAN R(

Donated by the author

THE

MONEY BELT

Outskirts Press, Inc.
Denver, Colorado

The Money Belt
All Rights Reserved.
Copyright © 2008 Alan Robertson
V2.0R1.1

Cover Photo © 2008 JupiterImages Corporation. All rights reserved - used with permission.

Outskirts Press, Inc.
http://www.outskirtspress.com

ISBN: 978-1-4327-2735-2

Outskirts Press and the "OP" logo are trademarks belonging to Outskirts Press, Inc.

PRINTED IN THE UNITED STATES OF AMERICA

For Evelyn

Special thanks to Whitley, Francey Rothschild, K.C. Meadows, Rick Leppanen, Tom Sima, Dan Leppanen, Mike Farrell, Eileen Leppanen, Joanne Spurr, Kelly Jacquez-Reynolds and Evelyn for your help and encouragement.

I returned, and saw under the sun, that the race is not to the swift, nor the battle to the strong, neither yet bread to the wise, nor yet riches to men of understanding, nor yet favor to men of skill; but time and chance happeneth to them all.

Ecclesiastes

Chapter 1

With a ready smile, outdoors look and deep blue eyes that conveyed more sincerity than he was actually capable of, Willie Salo was not without charm. And though a bit on the nervous side, after a few beers he could be easy-going and rather humorous. For these reasons, along with a greater than normal appetite for sex, there had always been women in his life. They would come and they would go and he never stopped to wonder why. So, when the real thing happened with Carmen, and then came to an abrupt end with her leaving him for someone of more substantial means, Willie did what he always did: rationalized, made a few wisecracks, then went on as though nothing of consequence had occurred. But it had, and he was no longer the same. He drank more, got high more and spent more time alone. And through the haze Willie began to see himself as others did—not the happy-go-lucky thirty-something bachelor of his imagination, but a loser hovering only a few microns above the plankton end of the food-chain.

As with many souls securely anchored to the economic bottom, Willie wanted better. A spiral notebook containing dozens of half-baked money-making schemes lay ready for action on his worn kitchen table. But that's where they ended: Just scribbles in a notebook. He was good at the dreaming part, but follow-through, *that* was Willie's shortcoming.

To be fair, most of his ideas were purely business in nature—ventures such as gopher ranching for meat and pelts, or home appliances powered by flatulence. And though some of his schemes fell squarely within the realm of illegal enterprise, Willie was not a criminal at heart. The cabin near Harlow Lake in Michigan's upper peninsula had been inherited from a distant uncle, and the old Ford pickup and his few other possessions had been honestly earned (mostly). And the idea of him masterminding a major felony, if mentioned to those who knew him, would be laughable. "He's a little odd," they'd say, "but okay."

But that all ended one idle Wednesday in early August when the garbage at the cabin reached critical mass and Willie was forced to haul a load to the county dump. While there he noticed what appeared to be an old money belt lying amid the mounds of detritus. Intrigued, he strode over to inspect it. Finding nothing inside its zippered compartment, but thinking the belt was kind of cool, he decided to bring it home.

Late that night, splayed across his kitchen table, bathed in the glow of a hissing propane lamp, the coal-black money belt became the focus of Willie's desperate desire to be more than he was, and the plan just fell together: Build a radio-controlled bomb in the belt. Strap it on someone with a load of cash. Then tell them to give it up or be blown to bits.

Good plan, thought Willie. And simple too. Wasn't much that could go wrong with a plan like this.

Chapter 2

Nine days later.

Morning sun steamed the last drops of dew from the rickety porch, and a gentle southern breeze swirled the scent of pine and moist earth through the forest air. After his second cup of coffee and well into his third cig, Willie determined it was time to get to work. Starting the small generator he used when he needed electricity (he was two miles from the nearest power line) he went inside to his tiny backroom workshop. An electronics repairman by trade, really more of a fix-it guy than true technician, he could usually ferret out a burned resistor or shorted diode, get some gizmo working again and make a few bucks on the deal. But his current project was, of course, something far different and much more exciting. A nervous wave swept over him as he unlocked the bottom drawer of a battered desk that served as his workbench and pulled out the money belt, now fat with explosives and electronic parts.

Inside the belt's money compartment he had installed some electronics from a garage door opener; a quarter stick of dynamite and blasting cap he'd won in a card game from a pipe-fitter who worked at the Tilden mine; the transmitter portion from one walkie-talkie (so he could listen to the subject continuously); the receiver portion from another walkie-talkie (so he could give him instructions); and several 9 volt batteries to power it all.

Additionally, the belt now featured a handy strap section which could be tightened but not loosened; and a clever new latch that, once closed, would not open again without his custom-made key. Without the key, and with the belt cinched tight, it would have to be cut off to be removed. Today he would install several thin wires extending from the buckle to the latch. The point was, if someone tried to cut the belt to remove it, wires would be cut. If the wires were cut it would trigger a voltage in a secondary circuit and fire the blasting cap in the dynamite. Thus, absent the key, once the belt was around someone's waist it was not coming off without a loud *ka-boom*.

Willie didn't for one moment think he could ever actually blow someone up, but for the plan to work he needed the threat to be real and credible. To that end, the belt had to be armed and the remote detonator had to work.

It took him a little under two hours to install the wires. When done, he connected a small buzzer to where the blasting cap would normally be. Then, snatching the garage door remote control from the desk, he punched OPEN and the buzzer immediately began a high-pitched *zzzzzzzzz*. Perfect, thought Willie. Absolutely perfect.

After a smoke break outside to settle his nerves, he removed the buzzer and installed the blasting cap and dynamite. Then, using more fine wire for thread, he sewed the zippered money compartment shut, soldered the zipper mechanism fast, and spread opaque rubber cement over its entire length. He felt these prudent physical measures, along with a suitably dire warning, would discourage anyone— most particularly the wearer—from trying to tamper with the belt to disarm it.

Now the new and improved money belt was complete and ready for action. Willie was overjoyed. And that, of course, that made him feel like partying. Problem was he'd spent the last of his cash on the previous evening's refreshments. So even though he didn't want to be bothered with such a mundane chore, he had to bring a guitar amp he'd repaired during the week to Bonello's Music Store in Marquette. The work would net him a hundred and thirty bucks cash—more than enough to satisfy his near-term needs. And while in town he could maybe call up his current girlfriend, Doreen Harmon, and smooth talk her into coming out to the cabin for drinks and perhaps other adult activity. It was Friday, and Willie wanted to party.

He gazed lovingly at the creation in his hands. Building it was the coolest thing he'd ever done. Then he pranced around the cabin, holding it in the air like a boxer with a title belt. It was special. He was brilliant. And for the first time in what seemed like an eternity, Willie had hope. And hope made him feel way too good to be straight. And that meant going into town to solve his cash problem. But what to do with the belt? After an internal debate marred by some ugly name-calling, he slogged toward the desk to put it away, but at the last moment hesitated, saying, "Ahhh! What the heck. Might as well take it with me." And so he did, carefully stashing it under the random accumulation of junk always present behind the seat in the old, green pickup.

Chapter 3

Doreen said, "No."

Willie make a sour face and stared at the receiver of the pay phone. "What do you mean, no? Come on, Doreen, don't you wanna have some fun tonight? It's Friday, girl, time to loosen up."

"I don't think so, Willie. Not tonight. I . . . I have plans."

"Plans? And your plans don't include me? I thought we had a thing goin'. Come on, hon, I got the hots for you big time. Don't make me suffer."

"Not tonight. I can't. Maybe next week."

"Next week! I could die from the swelling before then."

"I'm sorry, Willie, I just can't. I've got to go now. Janet is giving me that 'what are you doing taking personal calls during work' look. It'd be better if you didn't call me here at the bank. I could get fired. The new boss, Mr. Kramer, is very strict about this sort of thing. I like my job, Willie. I don't want to be a teller all my life. I want to be noticed. I want to get ahead. Don't get me in trouble. Why don't you call me at home next week and we'll talk."

Willie hung up. "Well, screw me. What the heck's going on here? Doreen acting all distant. Huh. Like maybe somebody else is pounding her pudding."

"Screw me," he said again as he climbed into his truck, started the engine and chugged up Front Street toward the music store.

After dropping off the amplifier and collecting his money, he rambled around town for a while taking care of errands, the most important of which was to lay in a substantial cache of beverage for the weekend. Then, more out of habit than plan, he drove north through town and out on County Road 550 toward the Harlow Lake turn-off and his cabin. But when he arrived at the turn-off, he didn't turn. What the hell, he thought, might as well cruise on up to the Squirrel, have a couple flat ones and see if anything's happening.

Chapter 4

A roadside tavern slightly more than half way between Marquette and the village of Big Bay thirty miles northwest, the Flat Squirrel bar squatted on property originally claimed by cedar and jack pine, and fiercely contested by swarming mosquitoes. The Squirrel had acquired its quaint handle during construction when a thirsty rodent lapped one too many sips of a workman's spilled beer. Later, lurching his way home, the poor critter failed to look both ways when crossing County Road 550. A critical oversight.

After the fully loaded logging truck rumbled past, the cute little tippler appeared as though he'd belly-flopped from 10,000 feet. A week of summer sun, coupled with the pounding pressure from hundreds of tires, rendered him paper thin and completely desiccated—though, remarkably, all his fur remained intact. Adding insult to injury, on the day the building was completed a carpenter with a sense of humor peeled him off the pavement and tacked him over the front door.

At the Grand Opening the tavern's two-dimensional namesake was ceremoniously carried in on a bar tray, duly certified as a happy customer, then stapled to the wall behind the bar for all to see and admire. And there was no denying it, the flattening process had created a unique work of art. For although the body was symmetrically spread-eagle, the head was turned in perpetual left profile—lips frozen in what one sober women described as a boozy wolf-whistle. Thus, for the relatively minor infraction of scampering while intoxicated, the hapless creature was sentenced to hang. A brass nameplate tacked below it identified the pelt as Sippy.

Later, in a stroke of marketing genius, the bar owner ordered special mugs wider than they were tall, and a pint of ale was thereafter known as a *flat one*. And from that day on, if someone said they were going out to "get flat," everyone knew they were headed for the Squirrel.

It was only 4:30, but it was Friday and the gravel parking lot was already filling up. Willie raised a light cloud of dust as he braked the Ford into a vacant spot.

Chapter 5

Eric Kramer closed and locked the door to his large, well-appointed office and changed from his dark-blue pinstriped suit into a fresh pair of crisply pleated khaki Dockers, tangerine polo shirt and fashionably worn deck shoes. Three times a week he worked out. Today was gym day. He would drive there directly from the bank. He never stopped to think about whether he would go or not. Once he'd made a decision to do something, he did it. Going to the gym Monday, Wednesday and Friday right after work was one of those things. He was fit and liked it: A healthy body being the ideal vehicle for a perfect mind. His gym bag with sweats, towel, shoes, jock and bottle of spring-water waited by the desk.

Leaving the bank with the other employees, he felt a sense of well-earned pride as one-by-one they said good-bye to him and wished him an enjoyable weekend. He smiled and returned their good-byes but made a point of not entering into any small talk. He wanted to keep his distance; to remain aloof. If he allowed them to get to know him personally it would decrease his leverage. And although there were some damn good-looking women working in the bank, he'd made a vow never to date any of them. It was about power. It was about control. Anyway, there were plenty of attractive and available women in Marquette.

Striding proudly toward the parking lot, Eric felt immediate pleasure when he saw that his new, slate-gray BMW 925z was parked in the President's spot. The odometer had recently turned 1,000 and he'd arranged for the dealer to pick it up for a post-break-in tune-up, with instructions to have it back in its parking space before four o'clock. Mattson's Cadillac, Mercedes and BMW, knowing which side their bread was buttered on with respect to inventory loans, had taken special care to do exactly as he'd asked.

Eric noted with contentment the smooth purr of the engine as he pulled out and joined a line of cars exiting the lot. He was behind a light-blue Toyota Corolla and recognized the driver as Doreen Harman, one of his tellers. With long coffee-brown hair, a good figure and great legs she'd sometimes show off in dresses slightly too short for business, she was attractive in a low-budget way. When it came to style and class she was not, and would never be, in the same league as the women he preferred. But she was someone who, under other circumstances—such as out of town at a banking conference—would be interesting for a night. He began to imagine how she would behave with him. He imagined she would do whatever he asked.

The Corolla pulled into the stream of traffic traveling north on Front Street and was gone. Eric mentally shifted gears and pulled into the traffic too. It was a beautiful afternoon. He was on his way to the gym for a workout, and after that to a birthday party for Annie Nancarrow at the Thunder Bay Club. Life was just about perfect.

Chapter 6

Willie opened the heavy wooden front door of the Flat Squirrel and was immediately assaulted by a thick cloud of smoke. With the practiced nose of a veteran honky-tonk sommelier, he noted a well-proportioned mixture of cigarettes, beer, sweat, perfume and marijuana. About forty men and women danced, laughed, drank and attempted to exchange relevant personal information in direct competition with a thousand-watt jukebox which was bludgeoning the audio spectrum with the blues-rock classic *Your Man's Gone Wrong*. Willie loved it! He started singing along as he made his way through the crowd toward the bar. *"Snuff out the God-damned light, and straighten up the bed. You can't make it on your charm this time, gonna have to use your head. 'Cause your luck's done gone. Your man's gone wrong."* The last word came out more like "rogg" as a huge hand closed around his throat. Willie struggled to keep his composure as blood flow to his brain slowed to a trickle and his lungs pumped frantically to recycle oxygen. His lips mouthed the name Moose, but the only sound that came out was a squeaky "ooohs".

Moose McCullough hadn't made the Dean's List in high school, but knew quite well that if he didn't let Willie go he would die—and that would almost certainly end the party. For his part, Willie did not struggle. It would have been pointless and merely prolonged the agony. Finally, predictably, Moose relaxed his grip and allowed Willie to breath.

"Damn, Moose, what'd you do that for? I thought we were friends?" croaked Willie.

Moose grabbed Willie's shirt, pulled him close and growled, "Friends don't come on to my girl."

Willie panicked—then recovered. "Are you kidding? I wouldn't do that. I'm not stupid."

"Sheila told me you were coming on to her the last time you were in here. You callin' her a liar?"

Oh Christ! groaned Willie, the old liar gambit. What an imbecile. But at two hundred sixty-five pounds—two hundred of it muscle—a lack of creativity in social gamesmanship didn't present any problem for Moose. And Willie really should have known better than to start putting the moves on Sheila. But it had been late and he had been well into his cups and Moose had been out of sight—perhaps outside puking, getting high or pulverizing some poor soul—and Sheila had looked good that night. She always looked good. And she was always giving him a glance that implied, "If Moose weren't around, we could . . ." And it was way back last month. And he'd estimated a month as the limit of Moose's memory and considered the Squirrel safe to reenter.

"Moose, listen. Sheila must have misunderstood me. I was just making conversation. We were talking about the Nature Channel or something."

"Humming birds," said Moose.

"Yeah. Yeah. We were talking about birds. Look, there's nothing wrong with that . . . is there?"

"She said you told her you could move your tongue faster than a humming bird could flap its wing, *and* you invited her out to your pickup for a demonstration."

"Man, I don't remember anything like *that*. She's *your* girlfriend. I wouldn't be crazy enough to say anything like *that* to her. Moose, she must have misunderstood. We were just talking about birds and stuff. Honest." And then in his most sincere tone, "I have *way* too much respect for both you and Sheila ever to come on to her. *Way* too much respect."

For nearly thirty seconds Moose didn't say anything. During this time it was all Willie could do to keep his mouth shut. It was a test. Whoever speaks first loses. And Willie did not want to lose because he'd seen the results of Moose's wrath before and absolutely, positively did not want to be on the receiving end.

Finally, Moose relented. "Okay, but watch it."

Knowing any spoken word could and probably would be

taken out of context and used as an excuse for mayhem, Willie nodded.

Moose turned and lumbered toward a table in the back. Willie could see Sheila there. She was staring at him. Oh, God! She was giving him *that* look. He tried to force his eyes elsewhere—the ceiling, the floor—but involuntarily they kept glancing back. He saw Moose arrive at the table. His huge head begin to swivel in Willie's direction. Sensing doom, a latent survival center deep within his medulla oblongata sprung to life, taking control of his body, spinning him like a dervish and bounding him toward the bar.

After two quick flat ones and a Marlboro his throat began to feel better. Regaining a sense of purpose, he casually panned around to see who was in the joint—all the while taking care not to let his eyes roam in the direction of Sheila and the beast. Then someone far more interesting caught his attention. Dark hair. Dark eyes. Golden complexion. Great body. It was *her*. Carmen. Sweet Carmen.

Willie and Carmen had been a major item for about a year before she suddenly dumped him and got hitched to Dick Hodges. Carmen was twenty-nine. Dick was in his sixties. Willie couldn't figure it out. Nevertheless, after the marriage Carmen put a lock on the honey jar and began treating him like a virus. He'd found that amazing because when they were together sex was like a drug they'd binge on till exhausted.

For several minutes Willie stared straight ahead in a Carmen-induced trance. Then a mental picture of hot Carmen getting sweaty with Dick Hodges flashed through his brain and caused an involuntary gag reflex. Turning back to the bar, he quickly downed the rest of his third beer to regain a sense of normalcy. The bartender was busy with another customer, but Willie caught his attention long enough to give him the squashing motion which signaled his desire for a refill. He knocked a fresh Marlboro from his pack and was about to reach into his pocket for a lighter but jumped when someone else's hand slid in before his.

Chapter 7

Workout over, Eric showered, dressed and strode out to the Beamer. He was on top of the world. The fine new car started instantly and soon he was whizzing past the 550 Store on his way to the Thunder Bay Club. But his good humor was not to last. It was only three miles further up the winding county road when he felt the heat on his right calf and gaped in disbelief at his carpet, which was melting in a most curious way around the drive train hump. *What the heck?* Eric slowed the vehicle and pulled to the shoulder just as sooty smoke began seeping through a gap in the rubber gearshift boot.

"Christ on a bike!" he shrieked, "My car's on fire!" And so it was.

The old saw, *Too many cooks spoil the broth*, had come to fruition earlier that day at Mattson's service facility when no less than five mechanics had been conscripted by owner, Teddy Mattson, from less important jobs to work on Eric's Beamer. You see, Teddy was in some financial difficulty, sales were slow and he was way overstocked. He knew he'd need financing to get him through the sales drought, and that meant going to Eric. He wanted to go to a happy, smiling Eric, not one who was scowling and grumpy. Therefore, it was vitally important to make sure the car went back to him in tip-top shape. Unfortunately, with so many men working on the vehicle, no single mechanic performed an entire task from start to finish, thus leading to one small but significant oversight: The wire leading to the electric choke on the carburetor was never reinstalled. This seemingly minor omission caused the choke to remain in the "on" position all the time; the result was an extremely rich gas/air mixture flowing through the engine. Although the engine *seemed* to run okay, much of the gasoline was still unburned as it left the cylinders, traveled thought the exhaust manifold, down the exhaust pipe and into the catalytic converter.

A catalytic converter is normally very hot inside, thus when the raw gasoline came into contact with the converter it ignited and burned with a fury. Soon the outside of the converter slash afterburner was cherry red. A few minutes later the intense heat from the glowing converter ignited the undercoating of the Beamer, and the rest is history.

"Christ on a bike," cursed Eric again as he stood fuming on the roadside. He wasn't at all mechanically inclined and didn't have the faintest idea what could have caused his BMW to spontaneously combust, but he *was* an expert at fixing blame, and the black finger of doom was pointing ominously at Teddy Mattson.

Chapter 8

Stepping out of the shower, Doreen carefully dried herself, then used the towel to dry the mist from the full-length mirror on the door. Stepping back she took stock of herself. She was twenty-eight, in good shape and wanted more out of life than a crummy teller's job and a part-time boyfriend who treated her like a blow-up doll. She wanted to live a little, see the world, buy nice clothes, go out to dinner at good restaurants and, most of all, she wanted to get married and have kids. Try as she might, she simply couldn't picture any of this happening with Willie. It wasn't that she didn't like him. She did. He was funny and sort of good looking and great in bed. But that was it. There wasn't any future in hauling Willie's ashes. She had to make a change.

Doreen had been moving incrementally toward this decision for a long time. Then, earlier in the day when he'd called, she'd reached the tipping point and said no. It was tough to do. After all, she was human too. She had needs and desires. But she had decided to put them away for a while to execute the bigger plan. No pain, no gain.

Doreen didn't know exactly how she was going to get what she wanted, but she did know it didn't involve playing naughty nurse for Willie or staying at home moping. So she pulled on a flower-print summer dress, found some matching tan sandals and a faux-pearl necklace for a touch of style, then walked purposefully out to her Corolla to begin her new life. The only problem was she didn't exactly know where to start. Almost all of her old girlfriends were already married. They had social events that only included other married couples. Single women were way too much of a threat to invite. It's not that the single woman would be out to steal their man, it's just that they hated to see their husbands make fools of themselves buzzing around the new girl at the party.

Men were so predictable, always thinking with the wrong head. Women knew what was important. That's why married women took control of social events. It eliminated problems which could crop up if the guest list were left to chance or whim. Doreen understood this—all women do. She'd do the same when it was her time. It was the smart thing. It was the right thing.

Nevertheless, she had to begin developing a new social life and she was determined to start immediately. She didn't have any illusions. She knew it would take time. She needed to meet people and make new friends. She would eventually find the right man.

After driving around Marquette rather aimlessly for the better part of a half-hour, Doreen decided she really didn't want to stop and sit in some dark bar while the sun was still shining on such a gorgeous afternoon. It truly was a beautiful day. Too nice to go home. Too nice to do nothing. So she finally decided to drive up to the stately Harbor Inn at Big Bay for a drink or two on the veranda and perhaps dinner. Who knows, she might actually meet someone interesting. And, if nothing else, she will have begun her new life.

Rolling her window down, she luxuriated in the soft, warm breeze that buffed her face and billowed through her sundress. She felt a bit reckless. She felt like Marilyn Monroe as she turned the Corolla north off Wright Street onto County Road 550 toward Big Bay.

Chapter 9

"Don't touch anything you don't plan on using," said Willie.

Carmen smiled mischievously. "Have you missed me, Willie?"

"Move your hand a little to the left and find out for yourself."

Carmen circled her free left arm around Willies waist and pulled in closer to him, purposefully pushing her breasts into contact with his back. She felt his muscles tighten. Her right hand moved deeper into his pocket. With the other hand she began to unbuckle his belt. Willie tried his best to remain casual. When the belt was loose, Carmen unbuttoned the button on his jeans. When Carmen's hand went to his zipper Willie knew he'd had enough.

"Jesus, Carmen! Have a little decency."

"Oh," she moaned in mock disappointment, "I just wanted to see if Little Willie's missed me."

"I just don't like to show off in public, Carmen. It makes other men feel so, ah . . . inadequate."

But Carmen wouldn't stop. She'd always loved teasing him and this was too much fun to quit. "Oh, come on, Willie," she cooed. "You've never been shy before."

Twisting far enough around to the right to disengage Carmen's hand from his zipper, Willie proceeded to refasten his pants and buckle his belt. With the fun over, Carmen withdrew her other hand from his pocket and chided, "No guts, no glory."

"So, what's up, Carmen? How come you're not home polishing Dickey's walker?"

"You don't have to be mean, Willie. Dick's out of town this weekend, and I was bored. It's been a long time since

I've been to the Squirrel. I wanted to see if any of the old crowd might be around."

"Yeah. I guess Dickey doesn't take you here too often, probably not enough ragtime on the jukebox."

"He's kind of a stay-at-home guy."

Willie took a sip of his beer. "So what's the deal, Carmen? You dropped me like a dead carp. Didn't even invite me to your wedding. That really hurt my feelings." He faked a pained expression.

"First of all, Willie, you don't have any feelings above your waist. And second, a girl's gotta think about her future. It wasn't anything personal. You know how I feel about you. It's just that Dick didn't like the idea of me seeing you anymore. Heck, I can't blame him. You'd do the same if you were in his shoes."

"So what do you guys do for fun? Organizing the 78's? Read Modern Denture? Play Yahtzee for Geritol? What?" Willie paused for effect. "Aren't you bored?"

Carmen scrunched her lips and tilted her head to the side. "Well, yes . . . I am bored. What's the use of being young and alive if you can't have fun?" She paused for a moment, then went on, "Oh, Dick's all right. He loves me, or something like that. But life with him is so predictable. And, I . . . sort of have to watch what I say. Especially around his friends. And I have to watch what I do. He gets mad if I drink too much. And I can't get high at all. He says I get too *provocative*." She wiggled her hips. "It embarrasses him. His friends whisper about us, and they joke about him behind his back. He's real sensitive about it. Knows it's happening. Then he comes home and puts a lot of pressure on me to be the ideal little wife. Tells me to act more reserved. To act proper. Act older."

"You're too much for him, Carmen. Shoot, I thought by now you woulda sexed him to death.

She shrugged her shoulders. "Can't pole vault with a rope."

Willie's eyebrows went up. "Dang, Carmen, you must be climbing the walls by now!"

"Pretty close."

"Listen, hon, I hate to see you suffer. Why don't you come over to Doctor Willie's clinic and we'll conduct an exam. I'm a specialist in these cases. I'm sure I can prescribe a line of therapy to relieve all that built-up tension."

"Oh, could you, Doctor?" she said, clasping her hands and feigning adoration.

"You bet! But things like this take time, Carmen. I don't think one treatment will be enough. You have a serious condition here. We'll probably need regular sessions over a long period of time."

"Oh, Doctor! Do you really think I could be . . . *normal* again?"

"Yes, my dear, I'm certain of it. But you must do exactly as I say or the treatment will be a failure."

Carmen moved closer and put her arms around his waist, purring, "What should I do first?"

Chapter 10

Passing the 550 Store and the parking lot at the trail-head to Sugarloaf Mountain, Doreen rounded a corner and was nearing the turnoff that led to a stretch of Lake Superior beach called Wetmore's Landing. Though she hadn't been there in years, it had been one of her favorite swimming and picnic spots when she was young. It was then she saw smoke pouring from under a car parked on the roadside a quarter-mile ahead. A tall, blond man was standing post-like twenty feet from the vehicle. Doreen tensed as she realized the car was a gray BMW and the man was her boss, Eric Kramer. Then she thought, Wow! Wait a minute. This is my lucky day!

Slowing the Corolla, she pulled to the shoulder behind the smoldering vehicle. A dozen thoughts passed through her mind in a matter of seconds, preeminent among them was, *Here's my chance to do a big favor for my boss, get noticed and chalk up brownie points.*

Scowling, Eric Kramer walked directly to the passenger door of the Corolla, opened it, grabbed Doreen's purse lying on the seat, tossed it into the back, climbed in and commanded, "I need a ride."

Geez, he's rude, thought Doreen, but she smiled and said, "Sure, Mr. Kramer. What happened?"

"Gosh, let's see, Doreen, I decided to light my car on fire knowing you'd be along any minute to help out."

Stunned, she stared at the smoking vehicle and then back at Eric.

"So, Doreen, think we could get moving? Or do you want to take some pictures first?"

Doreen put the Corolla in gear, then, giving wide berth to the Beamer, accelerated in the direction of Big Bay.

After driving in silence for several minutes, she mustered the courage to speak. "Where were you going?"

"Take me to the Thunder Bay Club." It was an order, not a request.

"Sure," she replied, "I'm on my way to the Harbor Inn. It's only a couple miles farther to the Club." As soon as she said "the Club" she felt like a fool. She'd never been to the Thunder Bay Club, very few locals had—save those hired as cooks, maids and maintenance workers. The "Club" was obviously not *her* "Club." There were haves and have-nots in the world, and "the Club" belonged to the haves. She could live her whole life in Marquette and in all likelihood never be allowed one foot inside the fence of the private, 1,000-acre compound complete with several small lakes, two rivers and dozens of luxurious cottages for its members.

"I'd be glad to drive you up there, Mr. Kramer." Then, after another interval of silence, added, "Too bad about your car. It's brand new isn't it?"

Kramer turned his face fully toward her and replied slowly, as if talking to a child. "Yes, Doreen, my car *is* brand new. But now it's on fire on the side of the road, and I'm late for an important engagement. But lucky me, *you* came along."

The icy chill in his voice made Doreen's heart sink. How could this have happened? I'm doing him a favor and he's acting as if it's *my* fault his car's on fire. Geez, how can things go so wrong? Then she remembered one of her grandmother's pet sayings, *No good deed goes unpunished.* The more she thought about the situation, the more she sensed that stopping for Mr. Kramer was not going to earn her any brownie points at the bank. As a matter of fact, it could work against her. Kramer would always associate her with the incident. In his stuck-up world this was a humiliation. Only peasants had cars that didn't work properly. Only lowlifes stood on the side of the road begging for help. This was an embarrassment to him—an embarrassment that she'd witnessed. Not only would he *not* be grateful to her for helping him, he probably wouldn't even want her around the bank anymore to tell the story of how she had helped poor Mr. Kramer when his junky car broke down. She saw her future at the First Northern National Bank of Marquette—it looked short and bleak.

Driving on, she passed Hogsback Mountain, Little Presque Isle and the turnoff she was so familiar with, the one to Harlow Lake and Willie's cabin. Emitting a quiet sigh, she wished she hadn't turned down Willie's proposition that afternoon. She wouldn't be in this mess now.

They drove on in silence. Time seemed to stand still. And though Doreen drove as fast as she dared, each mile seemed like ten.

"Do you have a cell phone?" asked Kramer in a hard, flat tone.

The sound of his voice made her jump. "What?"

Then in the slow voice, which not so subtly implied he was speaking to an imbecile, he again asked, "Do.... you.... have.... a.... cell.... phone?"

"No," answered Doreen.

"Stop at the next place with a phone," he commanded. "I need to make a call."

What a jerk! thought Doreen. She fought an urge to slam on the brakes and demand he get out. But she couldn't do it, she needed her job—if only till she could find another—so all she said was, "Okay. I think there's a place with a phone up another mile or two." She knew there was. She'd seen it many times, and even been there a couple times with Willie.

They drove on for another two minutes before she caught sight of it ahead on the left. It was the Flat Squirrel bar. Then, for the first time since she'd slowed for the burning Beamer, Doreen smiled. Eric Kramer was going into the Flat Squirrel. This was something she *had* to see.

Chapter 11

"**C**armen, what say you and I go out to my truck and talk this over? We could, oh, smoke a joint and ah . . . discuss your treatment."

"Hmmm, okay. But first I want to dance. Come on, Willie, let's dance."

"Dance? You know I'm not much of a dancer . . . unless it's the horizontal polka. Let's get a little high first, then I won't feel like such a fool."

Willie's protests were to no avail. Carmen was already dragging him through the crowd toward the dance floor, and he belatedly realized that dancing in public was the price he'd have to pay if he expected any poozle. Women are so cunning, he thought. Seeing his fate was sealed, he didn't resist.

Willie hated dancing. Nothing about it came naturally to him. When he watched women dance they appeared graceful; the motions effortless. Some of the men—a few— seemed natural too, but most appeared as though they'd ingested some hideous neurological toxin and had lost control of their limbs. Willie had some sense of rhythm, and based on that he surmised most of the men on the dance floor either didn't or the impulses from brain to extremities were so slow that they were chronically out of step. He thought he might be part of the latter group. How embarrassing. The only solution was to burrow as deep in the mass of dancers as possible so he wouldn't be seen.

Willie bumped, shoved and elbowed the couple into the center of the undulating crowd. Then, secure that he wouldn't be a sideshow for the onlookers, settled into some odd shuffling and twitching motions he felt might pass for dancing. There was absolutely nothing natural about it. He had to be constantly thinking about which limb to move next or all muscle activity would stop. He watched Carmen as she immediately began moving her feet, legs, pelvis, torso, arms, hands and head in a rhythmic, graceful, totally natural and extremely seductive manner. Watching Carmen dance, her eyes closed, head rolling, luxuriant black hair tossing from side to side, took Willie's mind off himself and reduced his misery index to bearable.

As the first song ended, Carmen threw her arms around him and gave him a long, grinding kiss. The feeling of her full lips on his signaled promise. Thinking this was good progress, Willie went with the flow. A new song started. It was the distinctive, raw tenor of Steve Winwood wailing about his need for a daily dose in the Spencer Davis Group's big hit from the past, *Gimmie Some Lovin'*. He noticed he and Carmen were now locked into the center of the dance floor by a fresh group of dancers. Carmen had tricked him into a second dance. Damn, he thought, I gotta get control of this situation.

When the song ended Willie grabbed Carmen by the hand and pulled her toward the hallway leading to the back door of the Squirrel. She didn't resist. Willie had paid his dues.

Chapter 12

Doreen pulled into the dusty gravel parking lot of the Flat Squirrel and, though it was nearly full, was able to find a spot near the front. Without speaking, Eric got out and began walking toward the entrance. Not wanting to miss the scene of prim Eric entering the workingman's paradise of the Flat Squirrel on payday, Doreen hurried to catch up.

Jogging to his side, she asked, "Ever been here before?"

"Not hardly," he snorted.

"It's a real friendly place."

"I'll bet."

Opening the heavy wooden door of the Squirrel, Eric surveyed the cacophony within. Things had picked up since Willie'd arrived. Nearly fifty dancers were crowded cheek to jowl in the small dance area. Girls and women from sixteen to sixty wiggled and writhed in an attempt at the latest dance move or simply to strut their stuff. Miners, lumberjacks, carpenters, plumbers, masons and laborers of every sort punished the floorboards with their heavy work-boots; gleefully waving their arms and stomping their feet as though the dance floor were covered with venomous snakes. *Gimmie Some Lovin'* was blaring out of the jukebox, and on the fourth beat of each measure the raucous crowd would pound their feet in an obvious attempt to cause major structural damage. The joists moaned and cried but held.

Eric peered through the haze for a pay phone. He spotted one hanging on the wall next to a table where a huge man sat with his arm around a chesty blond half his size. The blond was wearing a pink tank top which had obviously been chosen to display her abundance.

With effort, Eric worked his way through the crowd, edged sideways between two tables and finally reached the phone. He was now standing directly behind Sheila. For some unknown reason before dialing he turned momentarily to survey the room and, to his surprise, saw twenty or thirty pairs of eyes on him. He was used to attention, but not this much. Most of the eyes belonged to women. Why not? he thought. He was tall, sandy blond, handsome, athletic and wearing clean, expensive clothing in a bar populated by men who'd worked hard all day at dirty, difficult jobs, and looked it. By comparison, Eric, with his tangerine polo shirt and crisp Dockers, appeared as though he'd just stepped off the cover of GQ. He also noticed that men too were looking at him, some directly, others out of the corner of their eye. The looks were suspicious and unfriendly. To many of them, Eric was the prototypical enemy—someone smoother, handsomer, wealthier and more educated; with a better job, car and house; and a prettier wife or girlfriend. He was the kind of man who could take their woman away if he wanted to. They knew it. And he knew it. And they instinctively hated him for it—him and every other snotty, smart-assed, son of a bitch like him. They watched him carefully, and watched the eyes of their wives and girlfriends even more carefully to make sure they weren't checking him out. But some women couldn't help it, and some simply didn't care what their boyfriends thought. Sheila fell into both groups.

Chapter 13

Willie and Carmen made their way down the short hall to the back door. Once outside, Willie got his bearings and made a beeline for the Ford parked in the back row of the lot. They sat on the faded bench seat of the old, rust-on-green F-150 and began to smoke the last half of a joint Willie fished from the ashtray. The windows were rolled down and the cool, early-evening air felt good.

The two bantered and sparred for a while, then settled into an easy conversation.

"So, other than Doreen Harmon, what have you been into lately?"

Willie immediately thought of the money belt and felt an overwhelming urge to share his plan with Carmen. One of the reasons—probably *the* reason—Carmen had dumped him for Dick, was money. He thought of his dingy cabin, aging Ford and few meager possessions. His total net worth was probably no more than a couple thousand bucks. On the other hand, Dick Hodges was a successful businessman with piles of money, a large house and loads of expensive toys to play with. Next to Dick, he was just some loser with nothing to offer. But the money belt could change that in a day.

He knew he wanted Carmen, wanted her as much as he'd ever wanted anything. And, in a rare epiphany, realized if the plan worked out right he could have it all—the money, the good life *and* Carmen.

"Hey, hon, why don't you leave Dickey and come live with me."

"Huh!"

"I'm serious. Look, Carmen, you and I are made for each other. Ditch that guy and let's get back together."

"I'd do it in a heartbeat, Willie, but you know where I come from. I can't bear the thought of living my life out in some small dump, never having enough money, always wanting, seeing other people enjoying the good things life has to offer and knowing they'll always be out of reach." Carmen reached over and brushed a lock of his hair back. "I love you, Willie. You know I do. But love's not enough. I need a life too."

Willie understood. Carmen grew up on the south side of town. The side where the poor people lived. Her father was a part-time carpenter and full-time drunk. The family of six lived in a crummy, rundown, two-bedroom rental.

Carmen sat transfixed. She remembered shabby furniture and secondhand clothes, government surplus food and social workers; going to school and being shunned by the nice crowd. And when she left home at seventeen, vowed to never live like that again. Love was important, but poverty would grind away at it until there was nothing left.

Carmen was many things, but above all a realist. She understood her greatest asset was her looks. She also knew looks fade and chances don't come along every day. So when Dick Hodges began showing an interest, showering her with gifts and taking her places Willie never could, the practical side of her said, "This is it. This is the chance."

"Listen Carmen, if I tell you something, you think you could keep it secret?"

His voice tugged her back. "Sure. What is it?"

"I've got a plan. And if it works I'm going to have money. Lots of money. Enough to go anywhere and do anything. You could come with me. Have anything you want. It'd be great. Go to, say, the Keys or California or Mexico or France maybe, you name it. We could have some real fun."

Carmen was intrigued. "So what's this you're talking about Willie? Is it some invention?"

"Not exactly."

"Is it legal?"

"Not exactly."

"What? Some big drug deal or something?"

"No. This is more of a one shot thing. Either works or it doesn't. Either I'm a big winner or I just walk away. And there's hardly any risk. I've really thought this thing through, Carmen. I'm sure it'll work. And money . . . . We're talkin' *big* money."

"It's not legal, is it."

"Umm . . . not really. You know regular guys like me can't make real money legally. It's like everything's all fixed before you start. Some people have it and the rest of us don't. You can pick at the crumbs, but don't touch the cake. So, if you want it . . . really want it . . . you gotta take it."

Her face filled with concern. "You're not going to rob a bank or anything like that are you? Geez, Willie, you can't do that. You'll get caught. They'll send you to prison forever."

"No, hon, *I'm* not going to do it . . . Someone else is going to do it for me."

"Huh? Someone's going to rob a bank for you? How does that work?"

Until that very moment Willie hadn't actually thought of a bank as his ultimate target. He really hadn't thought much farther than the mechanics of the belt itself and the problems associated with controlling the subject while not getting caught . . . but a bank, yes, that would be the obvious target, because that's where the money is. He envisioned a huge vault crammed to the ceiling with cash. Small bills, large bills, old ones, new ones, piles and piles of money, cash, bills, bucks, dinero, dough, moolah, loot, scratch, lucre, swag, wampum, call it what you like; one million, two million, three, who knew how much money a bank might have on hand!

"Look, if I tell you about this thing, you've got to promise not to tell anyone else. This is big time. This is serious business, Carmen. It's probably my one and only shot at real money, the kind of money that sets a guy up for life, and I don't want anything to go wrong. And, I sure as hell don't want to get caught."

"Does anybody get hurt?"

"No, no one gets hurt."

"Okay, tell me. I promise not to breathe a word to anyone.

Willie knew it was true and decided it was time to roll the dice. "Carmen, if I had a lot of money would you come away with me?"

She thought for a moment, then answered. "Yes, Willie. Yes, I would."

That was enough for him. He relit the stub of the joint, took a drag, exhaled, then peacefully contemplated Carmen's beautiful face. He imagined the two of them on a boat, near an island where palm trees grow, sipping drinks decorated with colorful, miniature umbrellas and filled with the joy of the moment. Then he swiveled halfway around and swung his arm over the seat. After a few moments of digging he felt leather on his fingertips. Grinning with pride, he pulled out the belt and held it against the steering wheel.

Carmen didn't speak. Mouth open, she stared first at the belt, then at him.

"It's a bomb," said Willie.

Then she understood.

Chapter 14

Eric dialed the number for Annie Nancarrow's cottage at the Thunder Bay Club. The noise from the jukebox and raucous crowd made hearing nearly impossible, but piercing the din was the unmistakable *dah, dah, dah* of a busy signal.

"Damn," he muttered, hanging up. He waited, then checked the coin return for his quarters. Nothing. "That figures." Now he'd have to go to the bar and ask for change. As he turned away from the phone, there was Sheila standing directly in front of him. His eyes were drawn to her alluring face, then, involuntarily, they drifted further downward, surveying her remarkable, full breasts straining at the fabric of the flimsy cotton tank-top.

"Hard to hear with the jukebox going," she said. The area between table and pay phone was tight. Feigning need for space, Sheila moved forward and pressed against him. She knew fully well the impact her body had on men, and was determined to use it to her advantage. She wanted to talk to this guy, but first she had to immobilize him. From practice, Sheila knew the best way to do it was to press her body against his. She knew he'd like the way it felt. Men always did.

"Problems?"

"The line's busy and the phone took my quarters. You wouldn't happen to have change would you?"

"Not on me."

"Are you sure?"

"Do you see anyplace it could hide?"

Against his will, Eric again looked down at her breasts, then further, to Sheila's jeans. The jeans were stylishly faded and frayed, tight and perfectly fitted. They left absolutely no doubt that Sheila was a woman and there was nothing larger than lint in her pockets.

"I'd better go to the bar and get change."

"Look at that crowd," she said gesturing. "It'll take you forever. Why don't you have a seat with us? The waitress is bringing fresh drinks and she'll have quarters."

Eric appraised the seemingly impenetrable wall of inter-locked bodies between himself and the bar and realized Sheila was right. "Okay. Thanks, I will."

Sheila sat and motioned for Eric to sit next to her. A more unlikely trio couldn't be imagined—Moose, Sheila and Eric. Many of the women who'd been secretly, and not so secretly, watching Eric, now turned their attention to other matters. Everyone could see Sheila had him, and there was no competing with Sheila. The men turned away too, most with a sense of relief, but others with a tinge of pity for the blond fool who would all-to-soon say or do something to turn Moose McCullough against him.

"What are you drinking?"

"Ah . . . nothing thank-you."

"Oh, come on. I'll bet this is your first time in the Squir-rel and you've never tasted a chainsaw."

"Yes to both," replied Eric.

"Here," said Sheila, sliding a tall glass filled with ice and a clear liquid toward him, "try this. It's the house spe-cial. You'll like it."

Eric felt that not trying the drink would be rude. After all, the woman was going to give him change for the phone. Picking up the glass, he inspected it like a chemist, then sipped cautiously. "Hmm . . . It's good." he said, nodding.

Setting the drink on the table, he tried to slide it back, but Sheila wouldn't let him. "You keep it. When it gets this crazy in here the service is kind of slow so we usually order two at a time."

Eric noticed there were, indeed, four drinks on the table.

"I thought you told me the waitress was bringing you something?"

"I did. Every time she shows up with an order we make another one. It's easier than trying to flag her down."

Sheila took a long, slow sip of her drink. Eric involuntarily did the same. The cool spirits went down easily in the hothouse environment of the Squirrel.

"What's your name?"

"Eric . . . Eric Kramer."

"Well, Eric, it's nice to meet you, I'm Sheila." She held out her hand. He took it. It was soft and very feminine; the nails polished the same shade of pink as her top. He appraised her face and realized she wore almost no makeup. Sheila had a nearly perfect bone structure with soft smooth skin, and a natural color and beauty that didn't need any help—just a hint of pink on the lush, full lips, which she would from time to time seductively moisten with her tongue. Brushing back a stray lock of glowing blond hair, she gave him a mischievous smile. Her emerald eyes sparkled with excitement. At twenty-four and a woman in her sexual prime, she gazed at Eric as though he were the only man on earth. "Haven't seen you in here before. New around here?"

"I live in Marquette. And no, I've never been in here."

"I know. I'd remember." The way she said it left no doubt about her intentions. She said it as though Eric were a blond God who would never, could never, be confused with the mere mortals around him. She said it as though she were ready to give herself to him immediately; all he had to do was ask. Sheila could act this way because she had no fear. No fear of embarrassment or rejection or failure. Those things happened to others, not her. She was a master at the craft of being a woman. Her qualifications were beyond dispute. She'd been genetically endowed with a full, ripe body exuding sexuality and desire; and a clear, intelligent mind, unafraid of any sort of challenge or adventure. And she was still holding on to his hand; seductively rubbing her fingers against his palm.

For the first time in a long, long time, Eric stopped thinking.

"To new friends," she said, raising her glass.

"New friends," he responded, finishing the last of his drink and surprised it was gone. "It's good, what's in it?"

"No one knows. It's Big Jim's secret recipe." She nodded toward the bar. "He's the owner, and always makes a big show of turning his back to the crowd while mixing them, and he adds a splash of something from a pitcher he prepares alone in the back room. It's all very mysterious." Just then, the waitress—a plump girl with unruly hair coerced into a ponytail—weaved her way to the table with four fresh drinks.

"It's on me," offered the usually parsimonious Eric, pulling a twenty from his wallet and handing it to the waitress. "Could I have quarters with the change?"

The girl dug around in her apron, but all she had were pennies and bills. "Back in a minute with the quarters." She turned and began battling her way back to the bar.

"Another round too," called Sheila. "Make it six this time."

Nodding, the waitress disappeared into the seething mass.

"It'll only be a few more minutes. Is the call important?"

Eric sipped from the fresh chainsaw and casually tried to remember if the phone call was important. His thinking was getting fuzzy, but yes, the call *seemed* important—though perhaps not quite as important as when he'd first tried. The urgency was gone. He was feeling fine. He'd make it when the waitress brought the change. "Well, it seemed important," he replied. "I was supposed to be somewhere and had car trouble. I'm late and wanted to let them know why."

"Oh, too bad. Well, no sense worrying about what you can't change," said Sheila smiling.

"That's right," agreed Eric. The comment was so out of character he had to pause to think if he really meant it. He thought perhaps he did. In the short time that had elapsed since he'd entered the Squirrel his priorities had undergone a dramatic shift. Thinking didn't seem nearly as important as it had when he'd arrived—feeling seemed much, much more important.

"Let's dance," said Sheila.

A song with a pulsing beat thundered from the jukebox. Sheila, who was still holding Eric's hand, pulled him up and onto the dance floor, leaving Moose—who'd been completely ignored the previous fifteen minutes—smoldering alone at the table.

Chapter 15

Doreen couldn't believe her eyes. There, not twenty feet from her, was Eric Kramer, a smiling Eric Kramer, dancing with a blond ditz who looked as though her clothes had been applied with a paint gun. Life is so unfair, she thought. I work for him, stop and pick him up when he's stranded, drive him here for his precious phone call, and what do I get in return? Insults. Ignored. I'll probably even get fired. And now he's out there making time with some top-heavy bimbo who probably can't even count to eleven without taking off a shoe. The heck with him.

Pushing her unfinished drink away, Doreen wheeled around, forced her way through the crowd and out the front door of the Squirrel, found the Corolla, started it, paused long enough to turn her face toward the building and say, "Well screw you," then abandoned her plans for dinner and motored toward home.

She drove fast. And the more miles she put between herself and the Flat Squirrel the better she felt. As she neared Wetmore's Landing she decided to stop for a walk on the beach. Her nerves needed settling and the beach was the perfect venue.

Slowing the Corolla, she turned onto the sandy two-rut access road which wove through stunted jack pines for several hundred feet before ending in a makeshift parking lot. She left her car and, still in a huff, marched purposefully to the beach. Within seconds the majesty of the broad expanse of sapphire water and the calming effect of waves lapping the shoreline began to ease her anxiety.

What's really important here, she asked herself? Eric Kramer? No. My job? No. Willie? No. I've been spending way too much time worrying about people and situations that are only incidental to my happiness. Happiness can't be something someone gives you or takes away from you. It can't be as shallow as that? *I* can't be that shallow. I need to learn to be happy because of me, Doreen Harmon, and not be constantly waiting for someone, some *man*, to find me and make me happy. And, I can't expect some *job* to fulfill all my dreams. I may never *find* the perfect man. I may never *land* the perfect job. *Ever!* Does that mean I can't be happy? Shouldn't be? Don't deserve to be? Uh-uh. The happiness has to begin within me and radiate outward. It's a copout to rely on others. It has to start with liking who I am as a person, and thinking I'm decent and good and worthy of the good experiences life has to offer. Well, damn it! I am that person. And it's up to me to make today a wonderful day. I can do it. And if I can manage it on a day like today, the rest of my life should be a piece of cake.

Doreen kicked off her sandals and ambled barefoot along the clean white sugar-sand beach, pausing occasionally to watch a wave roll in. She walked as far as where a marshy creek drained into the lake, pausing to poke at some orange and yellow spotted touch-me-nots which snapped open at her slightest touch. She plucked a leaf from a sandbar willow, held it between her thumbs and made a whistle. Then picked three purple heart-leaf asters, braided the stalks together and left them slowly spinning in a tiny whirlpool.

Twenty minutes later, inner peace restored, she returned to her car.

"You know, it really is a fine evening," she said aloud. "I think I *will* go to the Harbor Inn for dinner."

Chapter 16

Sheila's body moved seductively to the beat of the music, occasionally bumping and rubbing against Eric. She had him totally sensitized to her touch. She could feel him flex when she touched him—feel him harden his muscles the way men do when they want to impress. He looked good to her. The only question remaining was what she would do with him. She was feeling fine. The chainsaws, the pounding rhythm of the music and the close proximity of Eric were all working in seductive harmony. As she danced she began to imagine making love to him. Taking him inside and moving with the rhythm until the final, indescribable release. She knew she was ready. And from the way his eyes followed her every move, she knew he was too.

As the song ended Sheila pulled Eric close and whispered, "Let's get out of here." Then she took his hand and led him back toward the table to collect her purse and leave.

Hot from dancing and dizzy from the low oxygen level in the Squirrel, Eric saw his drink and drained it. Setting the glass down, something shiny caught his eye. Quarters. The quarters seemed to have some significance. What was it? Then he remembered Annie Nancarrow and the phone call and felt a jolt of adrenalin. No matter what he did tonight he *had* to make that call, and he'd better make it now. Grabbing two quarters from the table, he turned and rammed them into the pay phone, dialed the number and one ring later was talking to Annie.

Sheila was taken back when she saw Eric go to the phone. Moving close as possible, she listened.

". . . had car trouble . . . I'm at the Flat Squirrel . . . Of course I want to come . . . Wanted to call to let you know I'd be late . . . Who? . . Ray! . . Annie, I wish you'd told me . . . I'll be there as soon as I can."

Sheila was watching Eric's face closely and didn't like what she saw. Somehow the phone call had changed him, undone her work; broken her spell.

Turning to her, Eric said, "I've got to go."

"Go? Go where?"

"The Thunder Bay Club. It's very important. I'm supposed to be at a party there tonight. I just found out the chairman of the board of my bank is flying in. I can't miss it. He wouldn't understand. I . . . I can't miss it. I've got to go."

Eric's eyes scanned the bar for Doreen. He'd left her over half an hour ago. Where was she? The layout of the Squirrel was an L shape. They were at a prime table near the corner of the L. Stepping up onto his chair, he could see just about everyone in the place. No Doreen. She was either in the ladies room, outside, or she had left. "If she's abandoned me," he growled, not finishing the sentence.

Several feet to the left of the phone was a window. Eric squeezed his way past a table of revelers and peered out toward where he knew Doreen had parked her small blue car. The space was empty.

"Damn it!" he said, pounding the wall with his fist. Turning around, he squeezed his way back to where he'd left Sheila.

"Can you give me a ride?"

"Where?"

"The Thunder Bay Club."

"Sure," she said, face brightening. "Take me to the party."

Eric snorted a laugh. "You're joking."

Sheila moved closer, pressed herself against him and whispered, "Take me."

"Look, ah . . . Sheila, you just wouldn't fit in."

"What?"

"I mean, the guests there are bankers and business people. It's not the Flat Squirrel. Nobody falls down drunk, does the shimmy or urinates off the porch. I don't think you'd feel comfortable."

Hearing the last sentence, Sheila froze. Then her warm

smile melted into something less pleasant. She understood exactly what he meant. She would have been good enough to have sex with, but nowhere near good enough to show off in public. She took a half step back and slapped him hard across the face. "Get your own ride."

"Bitch!" snarled Eric.

Sheila swung again, but this time he parried the blow, causing her to fall sideways. As she did, her other hand arced out and caught Eric by the V in his polo shirt, ripping it as she broke her fall.

"Get your hands off me!" he shouted, yanking her wrist away from his shirt. "Look what you've done!"

Sheila was in shock. In her entire life no man had ever expressed any desire for her *not* to touch him. Regaining her balance, her eyes met his and all she saw was contempt. She began to speak, then stopped as a cold smile crossed her face. The smile became sweeter as she turned to the table where they'd been sitting—and to where a hair-triggered, one-man wrecking crew remained.

"Moose honey," she said in a sugary little-girl voice, "this guy's bothering me."

The words were sweet music to Moose McCullough's ears. His thick facial features slowly morphed into a sardonic smile. Rising, he clamped a vise-like hand on Eric's shoulder. "I think you and me should go outside and have us a little talk."

Eric replied, "You and I have nothing to talk about."

"I say we do," said Moose, squeezing.

Eric rolled his shoulders, twisting and dipping as he did and, miraculously, freed himself from the powerful grip. Backing up a step, he puffed himself up. "Do you know who I am? I'm Eric Kramer, president of the First Northern National Bank."

Moose was singularly unimpressed. He had no need for a bank. In fact, he'd never been in one. Most of his money was spent on Sheila, or at the Squirrel, or places like it. The rest, if there was any, was left on his kitchen table. No one in their right mind would ever be stupid enough to take Moose

McCullough's money. Everyone, including the petty criminals who preyed on the locals, knew that for their own health
it was far better to leave Moose's possessions alone. Even
local law enforcement officers gave Moose wide berth. One
night four of them had tried to take him in on a drunk and
disorderly charge. Three suffered minor injuries and the
other backed off. After a brief period of reflection they
called off the arrest, rationalizing that Moose's presence on
the street performed a peacekeeping function. And to a certain extent it was true. If a fight started, Moose would want
to get in on the fun. But, of course, once Moose became involved no one else had any fun. Therefore, most disagree-
ments in his general vicinity tended to be settled quickly and
quietly, with both parties agreeing that to walk away unsatis-
fied was infinitely better than to be hauled away unconscious.

"Well, mister banker man, I think I'm gonna make me a
deposit." With that, Moose grabbed a handful of Eric's once
smart tangerine polo shirt and hoisted him off the floor. The
assembled crowd, keenly aware of pending mayhem, automatically parted, clearing a direct path to the rear exit from
the place where Moose stood holding the president of the
First Northern National Bank aloft.

Moving with a quickness that belied his size, Moose
hustled Eric across the dance floor and down the hall, kicked
open the back door and sauntered out onto the rail-less back
porch. To the right was a dumpster. Straight ahead, down a
flight of four wooden steps, was the gravel parking lot. To
the left were stacks of empty wooden beer cases. He paused
to think, but only for a moment. Then, using his extraordi-
nary strength, he lifted Eric high in the air, took a step to the
right and tossed him head first into the large, green, foul-
smelling dumpster. Moose huffed a satisfied laugh, strolled
down the steps and watched patiently as Eric groveled to
right himself in the soggy garbage. As Eric's head appeared
from the dumpster Moose's patience expired. He caught the
banker with a hard right that landed flush on the jaw.

Mass times velocity equals power. The laws of physics

are fixed and immutable. The fist, forearm, bicep, shoulder and entire forward-going part of the body all constitute the moving mass of a punch. That Moose had exceptional mass in his punch was never in doubt, but it was the quickness of his reflexes which made him truly potent. Mass times velocity had just turned out Eric's lights. How long he would sleep in the moist, spongy womb of the dumpster was anyone's guess.

Casually flipping the lid closed, Moose swaggered up the steps to the back door of the Squirrel, certain a hero's welcome lay within.

Chapter 17

Willie and Carmen watched the whole thing. As Moose disappeared into the Squirrel, Willie glanced at the dumpster and let out a sigh of relief, thinking, But for the grace of God, there go I.

"Did you see that! Do you know who that is!" cried Carmen. Without waiting, she answered her own question. "That's Eric Kramer!"

"Huh?"

"The guy Moose McCullough just threw in the garbage is Eric Kramer. He's the president of the First Northern National Bank."

Willie and Carmen looked at each other, then at the dumpster, then their eyes converged on the belt.

"He's the one, Willie. He's the one you want to put the belt on. Think about it! Who better? He can walk right into the bank, walk right to the vault, grab a couple bags of money and walk out again without anyone asking a question. Who would dare? He's the *president* of the *bank!*"

Willie's world started to spin and his mouth went dry. Oh, God! It was one thing to talk about doing it. Even building the belt into a bomb, well, that was all academic, nothing illegal, or maybe just a little bit illegal. And to dream of doing it, and getting the money and getting away with it, well, yes, that was all fine and good. But to do it, to really do it, to push all his chips on the table and risk everything on this one hand, knowing if he lost he'd be losing big time, for a long, long time. Oh, Jesus! That was something altogether different. His eyes went to the belt; then to Carmen. "You'd really come with me?"

"Damn straight!" said Carmen. Then added, "Opportunities don't come along every day, Willie. When they do you need to take advantage of them. Let's do it, Willie. Let's do it and do it smart; then leave here and live like royalty. No more scratching for a living. No more yes sir, no sir to the people who control your life. No more wanting for the basic things that make life nice. Oh, God! Willie, let's do it. I'm so tired of Dick and his smarmy, stick-in-the-mud friends. And I'm damned tired of having to ask permission. You know, Willie, a couple million dollars means never having to ask permission again. We'd have money. We'd have fuck you money, enough to say fuck you to anyone who bothered us and not have to worry about it. Just think. We could get a big boat and sail around the world. Or, if we found an island we liked, with white sand beaches and warm surf washing the shore, we could just buy a place and stay there. We could do anything we want! Do it, Willie. Put the belt on him and let's get rich."

"Do it," he replied weakly. But he didn't move.

"Look, Willie, the best part is he's unconscious. He can't *see* you! And when he wakes up he won't know who put the belt on him. Then he'll have to do what he's told or else." She paused, glanced toward the bar, then turned back to him and continued. "We've been out here for nearly a half-hour and no one's seen us. Other than Moose and the banker, no one's been back here at all. Who saw you in the bar? Me, Moose, Sheila, the bartender, anyone else who knows you?"

"No, I guess that was all."

"Same for me. I arrived just before you did. I think Moose and Sheila saw me, they see everybody who comes in the place. And the bartender too, but that's it. There wasn't anyone else in there that I knew. You and I left together nearly a half-hour before Moose tossed mister bank president into the dumpster. If anyone asks, we can say we went to your place, or out to Little Presque Isle, or some place else to have a couple of beers and talk about old times." Carmen looked at the belt and asked, "What's the range on the walkie-talkie?"

"About a quarter mile."

"Go over there and put the damn belt on him and let's get out of here. We can drive down 550 and turn off on one of those old logging roads and hear him on the walkie-talkie when he wakes up."

Willie's hand was shaking as he reached for the door handle.

Chapter 18

Outside, next to the truck, his legs were like rubber and he could barely stand. He was as nervous as he'd ever been in his entire life. It was too soon. He hadn't worked out all the ramifications of the plan yet. Something this big had to be thought through, otherwise there were bound to be mistakes . . . goof-ups . . . blunders . . . things you'd look back on later and say, "The flaw was *so* obvious. How could I have been that stupid?" He wanted desperately to go back to the cabin, open a beer, smoke a big fat doobie, then pull out his pen and paper and list all the things that could possibly go wrong, just to make sure he'd covered all his bases and tied up any loose ends. And to sit and think and think and think for at least a couple of long, languid days—or at bare minimum a six pack or two—before committing to doing this thing: a thing that once in motion could never be undone. Willie unconsciously began to babble. "Act in haste, repent at leisure. Act in haste, repent at leisure. Oh, sweet Jesus!"

Fighting against this tide of self-doubt was the growing awareness that Carmen was right.

When would I ever get another chance to put the belt on someone without them knowing it was me, he thought? Someone who could waltz right past the guards and tellers and use his own keys or combination or whatever they use to open up the vault and just shovel out the money. Someone who could actually unlock the front doors of the Bank and then go to the vault and, with no pressure from alarms or cops or guns or anything whatsoever, fill up a big bag with money and walk right out. And if anyone asked him about it he could make something up, or just tell them to shut up because it wasn't any of their business and get back to work and don't ever bother me again or you're fired, but first go get my car and pull it around front 'cause I've got this big heavy bag of money and I've got a real important place to go to with it on important business of the kind which you wouldn't understand so get your ass moving right now or you're fired. A bank president. Where would he ever get another chance like this? A bank president in a dumpster!

Then the mental image of that sissy banker snoozing in the trash not fifty feet away caused a laugh to burst out of his throat like a gas bubble. Embarrassed, he glanced back inside the truck and saw Carmen in a highly agitated state. Her lips were mouthing the words *"GET MOVING!"* and she was jabbing her finger in the direction of the dumpster. Oh, God! Oh, God! he thought, and then realized his feet were moving . . . moving toward the dumpster . . . faster and faster.

Willie started to run, then braked back down to a fast walk. He looked around for about the twentieth time. There wasn't anyone outside to see him and the back of the Squirrel didn't have any windows, but if someone *did* see him he didn't want to call any particular attention to himself by running. "Just walk over there quickly and do it," he said to himself. "Get to that dumpster, open it up, whip the belt on that sorry sucker and get back to the truck on the double. Then get the hell away from here."

Long before he really wanted to be there, long before he was mentally prepared to be there, he was there. Stopping short, he surveyed the dumpster, nodding with odd satisfaction when he noted it was a Dempster. Then, walking around it, he checked it out as though it were a classic car—all the while letting his eyes roam the parking lot to make sure no one was watching. When his gaze landed on his own truck, he saw Carmen pounding on the glass and mouthing words he could only guess meant *"Get your ass moving!"*

Going around to the front, he opened one of the two lids. Looking in he saw Kramer, still in la-la land, cozied up in a foot of wet, stinky garbage. It was now or never.

After getting out of the truck, Willie had somewhat comically wrapped the belt around his own waist, holding it together in front with one hand. Having the belt around his waist seemed less conspicuous than carrying it. He didn't want some casual observer, who'd otherwise not have given him a thought, to wonder what he had. Now he took it off and reached into the dumpster to fasten it around Eric Kramer's waist, but Kramer was too far in and he couldn't reach him. "Oh, Christ!" moaned Willie. He closed his eyes, sighed, opened his eyes, puckered his lips, glanced around one last time, then scrambled over the side and into the dumpster with Eric.

Once in, he ducked below the level of the rim so no one happening by could see him. Looking around, he realized how filthy the walls were and made a mental note not to rub against them. Not wanting to lean over and risk fouling a knee in the gooey mess, he duck-walked himself into a straddle over Eric and began putting the belt on him. But it was tough going. Eric was lying on his side in a semi-fetal position, and he was heavy. Willie tried sliding the belt under him, but it wouldn't go. Frustrated, he grabbed Eric by his own belt and, with effort, was able to pull his waist high enough to scoot the money belt between him and the garbage he lay on. That done, he gently lowered Eric back into his gelatinous bed. Then Willie clasped the money belt shut and slowly pulled the strap tight. He pushed and pulled on the belt some more to make doubly sure it was around the smallest part of the stomach area and again pulled the strap tight, taking up the last bit of slack. The last pull caused Eric to twitch to life. His hand moved up to his face. Alarm bells went off in Willie's head and he froze. Eric's hand brushed absently at a fly that had been checking out one of his nostrils, then, with the fly gone, tucked itself back under his cheek. Willie stayed absolutely still for a long ten count, then he began to rise. As his head breached the level of the rim he was again gripped by panic—*the back door of the Squirrel was opening!* Immediately Willie ducked down as low as he could so as not be seen. He heard someone come out, walk down the steps and head directly toward the dumpster. In his mind's eye he could see the newspaper headline—LOCAL

CRIMINAL CAUGHT IN DUMPSTER STRAPPING BOMB ON BANKER! Willie held his breath. Then he heard the unmistakable sucking and blowing sounds of someone smoking a cigarette. Oh no! he thought. He's gonna stay right here and smoke that whole damn thing! That'll take ten minutes. Oh, screw me!

Willie was bent over in a deep crouch straddling Kramer and trying desperately not to move. The position was totally unnatural and hideously uncomfortable. In less than a minute his thighs, calves, back and butt muscles were all twitching uncontrollably, every cell exhausted and screaming for mercy. Adding to that, the stink in the dumpster was horrible and Willie found himself starting to gag. He was trying with all his might to stifle the gag reflex when a cramp sprang to life in his right foot. He felt his toes begin to curl under and the pain became unbearable. He gritted his teeth as tears welled in his eyes. He *had* to move his foot! Then he heard the back door open again and someone say, "Let's not take all day, okay?" He recognized the voice as that of Big Jim, the owner of the Squirrel. The smoker replied, "Okay, Jim. I'm coming right now." He saw a quarter of a cigarette fly into the dumpster, carom off the wall and land in Eric's hair. Instantly the hair around the glowing butt began to twist and smolder. Willie didn't want to move because he hadn't heard the employee go back in the door yet, but if Eric's hair caught fire it was a sure bet he'd wake up. "Oh God, why?" moaned Willie. Then he heard the employee walk back up the steps and open the door. When the door banged closed, he breathed a sigh of relief, grabbed a handful of rotting lettuce pulp and gently patted it into Eric's hair, extinguishing the cigarette. The pain from the cramp was now beyond description and Willie's leg muscles were so tight he could barely rise, but he knew if he didn't get out of the dumpster at once he was going to barf. Lifting his eyes above the rim and seeing no one, he pulled himself upright. Then, with enormous effort, he hauled himself out of the dumpster, straightening his kinked muscles as he did. Standing semi-upright on the ground he turned to leave but, remembering something, turned back and dove half way into the dumpster, staying there for several seconds balancing on the rim with his legs wiggling in the air while he reached in and pressed a hidden switch that activated the belt. Done, he kicked and squirmed his way out of the dumpster again, paused for a short moment to see if anyone was around, closed the lid as quietly as he could, then made straight for the Ford. Slime covered his hands to his elbows, and his running shoes made squishing sounds as he limped like a hunchback toward the truck.

"Did you do it?" asked Carmen as Willie slid in, pulling the door closed behind him.

"Damn straight, baby. Nothing to it."

"Then let's get out of here."

"Right on," said Willie. But when he tried to turn the key to start the truck his hand was shaking so badly Carmen had to do it for him.

Chapter 19

Luck was with them. No one was outside as Willie and Carmen drove out of the parking lot and hung a right on 550 toward Marquette. Once on the highway, Willie accelerated to exactly fifty-five miles per hour. He desperately wanted to put distance between them and the Squirrel but didn't want to risk a speeding ticket this close to the scene of the crime.

"Over there on the left. Turn off there," cried Carmen.

Willie saw the old two-rut road that led north-easterly toward Lake Superior; most likely to some seldom-used lake frontage. Taking care to use his turn signal, he slowed and made the turn. He wondered about his brake and signal lights. He hadn't checked them in a while—most likely never—and didn't want to get stopped for having a light out.

"Drive out of sight of the road and then turn around and park," Carmen instructed. "Then we can start listening."

Willie did as he was told. He noticed the road didn't appear to have been used in some time. The grass was tall and unbent, and thin saplings were growing on the median. He found a spot to turn the truck around, did so, stopped and shut off the engine. They were about a hundred feet from the main road and wouldn't be seen or heard.

Willie reached behind the seat and came up with the receiver/walkie-talkie/garage door opener combination all duct taped together to form one unit. Switching the receiver on, he turned the volume up to full. Nothing. Either Eric was still snoozing or the damn thing wasn't working. He keyed the mike on the walkie-talkie, thought for a moment, shrugged his shoulders and then yelled, "WAKE UP!" They waited. Nothing. "WAKE UP!" he yelled again. Then he and Carmen heard the unmistakable sounds of someone coming to.

"Wha . . . Wher . . . Whas . . . Ugghh . . . Whas that smell? . . Oh, God! . . . Oh, my face . . . Where am I? . . Let me out of here! . . . Let me out of here! . . . *LET...ME...OUT...OF...HERE!*" Eric was screaming and pounding on the wall of the dumpster.

"Willie, you've got to shut him up before someone hears him. Talk to him, Willie. Talk to him."

Willie stared at the walkie-talkie as if seeking inspiration, then keyed it and in an obviously phony *basso profundo* commanded, "Shut your mouth unless you want to get blown up."

"What? Who's there?"

"Shut your damn mouth and listen to me. Do exactly as I tell you and I'll let you live," he said, feeling a surge of power.

"Okay, who are you? Let me out of here?"

"Don't you understand English? I told you to shut your mouth."

"Okay."

"You're in a dumpster. Push upward on the lid and climb out."

Willie and Carmen heard the sound of the lid opening and the scraping, bumping sounds of Eric clambering out of the dumpster.

"Christ on a bike! I'm filthy."

"Shut your mouth if you want to stay alive," ordered Willie, anger rising in him. "Do exactly as I command and maybe, just maybe, I'll let you live."

Eric didn't say a word.

"Do you see that belt around your waist?"

"Of course I see it," came the testy reply.

"It's a bomb." He paused for emphasis, then went on. "Don't bother trying to take it off. It won't come off without exploding. Don't pull on it or cut it or tamper with it in any way. Do you understand?"

"Yes, but . . . "

"But what?"

"How do I know it's a bomb?"

"There's only one way to find out," said Willie. "Mess with me and I guarantee you'll find out in the worst possible way. I'll blast you to smithereens you punk. And when they scrape up what's left they won't be able to tell your lips from your spleen. Get the picture?"

"Yes," came the timid response.

"Good. Now we're making progress. I want you to look around. Is anybody there? Is anybody watching you?"

"No."

"Did anybody see you get out of the dumpster?"

"No, I don't think so."

"Good. Now . . . do you see where the back of the parking lot ends and the trees are?"

"Yes."

"Walk through the parking lot into the woods till you're far enough in so no one can see you. Do you understand?"

"Yes."

"And tell me when you get there."

"Okay."

Willie and Carmen heard the crunching sound of footsteps on gravel.

"Run!" commanded Willie.

The sound turned into a run.

After several seconds, Eric said, "I'm here."

"Good. Did anyone see you?"

"No, I don't think so."

"Good. Now listen closely." Willie paused to think of what to say. He'd never thought it out quite this far and didn't have a script. "Okay. You will walk out of the woods and go directly to your car. You will . . ."

"But . . ." interrupted Eric.

"Shut your goddamn mouth and listen to me or I'll push the button right now and blow you to pieces. Do you understand?"

"Yes."

He began again, "You will walk out of the woods and go directly to your car. You will drive to your house in Marquette. You will clean yourself up. Then you will drive to the bank and get . . . ah . . . five million dollars. As you leave the bank I will give you further instructions. Once I have the money I will tell you how to safely take the belt off. But remember, I push one small button here and you're a dead man. Try to take the belt off yourself, you're a dead man. And one final thing, if I don't personally deactivate the bomb within twenty-four hours, it blows up on its own. And, as you already know, I can hear every word you say. Try to call the cops, I blow you up. Understand?"

"Yes."

"Any questions?"

"Yes, a couple with logistical significance and one purely personal."

"Well what?"

"The personal one first," he said. "How do I know you won't blow me up anyway after I get you the money?"

"Simple. You've never seen me and you never will. I have absolutely no reason to kill you. And, most importantly, I want the belt back. See, pal, you get the money. I tell you where to drop it. Then I tell you to go someplace else. When you get to the other place and I have the money, I tell you how to get the belt off without blowing up. If you try to take it off without my help you'll trigger the bomb and kill yourself. But I can tell you how to get it off safely. And once you have it off, you better run like hell, because I'm gonna blow it up."

"I thought you said you wanted it back?"

"I do, you moron, but only to blow it up and get rid of the evidence. What's it to you anyway? Nobody is going to blame you for this. You're an innocent victim. The bank's insured isn't it?"

"Yes, of course."

"Well then? What's the problem? You're not going to lose a thing. Monday morning you'll be back on the job screwing widows and orphans, and I'll be long gone. So get your sorry ass moving and do what I say."

"I said I had a couple logistical questions. Can we talk about them? They're important."

"Okay, what?"

"First of all, I don't have a car. My car broke down on 550 by Wetmore's Landing and someone gave me a ride here. But now she's gone and I don't have any way to get home."

"What happened? Your date leave while you were napping in the dumpster?"

"Very funny. I don't know. She just left, that's all. She's gone and there's nothing I can do about it. So how am I supposed to get home? I'm covered in stinking slime and wearing a bomb. Who in their right mind is going to give me a ride? Huh? Who? . . . Why don't *you* give me a ride home?"

"Listen, pinhead, don't get cute. You really don't want to see me, because if you do then I have no choice; I *have* to blow you up."

"You have a good point there."

"Damn right I do."

"Okay . . . . So what do you suggest?"

"I don't know. I gotta think about it a minute."

"There's one other problem."

"What?"

"All of the bank's cash is kept in the vault overnight."

"So?"

"The vault has a time lock on it and can't be opened till nine o'clock tomorrow morning."

Willie didn't key the mike. "Oh, shoot!" he groaned. "I should have thought of that. Of course there's a time lock on the vault."

Carmen looked at him and shrugged. "Just tell him to go home and stay there. And don't answer the door or the phone. Also tell him he should get dressed and go to work tomorrow morning like nothing's happened and get the money and then you'll give him further instructions."

"Did you hear me? I can't get into the vault now because there's a time lock on it."

"Yes, I heard you."

"So what do you want me to do? Come on. The mosquitoes out here are terrible."

"That's what you get for playing in the dumpster."

"You're a real funny guy."

"Listen, douche bag, I'm not the one festooned with garbage and wearing a bomb."

"I see your point."

"Okay then."

"Okay what?"

"Huh?"

"What?"

"What what?"

Eric's frustration was mounting. "Exactly what do you want me to do mister bomber? I don't have a ride. I can't go into the bar and ask for one, and I can't go out to the road and flag someone down."

Willie had an answer. "Steal a car."

"WHAT!"

"I said steal a car from the parking lot and drive it home."

"You're joking?"

"I'm *not* joking. Get your ass out there and steal a car!"

"How?"

"How do I know how? Just get out there and do it!"

"Listen, I'm a banker, you're a criminal. I don't know how to steal a car. You do. So you need to tell me how."

"Look here, chump, I'm a bomber not a car thief."

"What? Are you in a union or something? You're telling me you've never stolen a car?"

"That's right, I've never stolen a car. I'm a crazed bomber, not a petty car thief. But *you*, *you're* going to steal a car right now. And then you can tell me all about it. Then we'll both know. Think of it as job security. You'll have a back up trade in case the bank gig ever goes belly up."

"Oh, that's hilarious."

"Listen, clown, you don't wanna piss me off. My finger's on the trigger that controls your destiny. *I am your controller!* And if you know what's good for you you'll hustle your sorry ass out into that parking lot right now and steal a car."

"You still haven't said how?"

"How? How do I know how? Just look around till you see a car with the keys in it, then get in and drive away. That's how."

"Nobody's stupid enough to leave their keys in their car."

"Of course they are. Lot's of people leave their keys. I do it all the time. Take a look. You'll see."

"You leave your keys in your car?"

"Are you friggin nuts? I'll give you till the count of three to get moving. One . . . Two . . ."

"All right, all right, I'm going. But I still don't think it'll work."

Rolling his eyes in exasperation, Willie turned to Carmen. "This guys an imbecile. Can you believe he runs a bank?"

"Yeah, geez Willie, lucky you got control of him right away or the conversation could have dragged on. Toward the end there I thought maybe you were going to invite him over for dinner; have some drinks, meet the in-laws, you know, really get acquainted before the wedding."

"Ho, ho, Carmen, you're a riot."

"I'm just saying you gotta keep this thing short and sweet. You don't want him to get to know you. Know what I mean?"

Willie felt foolish. She had a point. He had to get control of the situation. "Christ! Now we gotta baby-sit him all night so he doesn't start getting ideas. And he seems like the kind of guy who'll try something. Especially if he's home and feels comfortable."

"Maybe we shouldn't let him go home too soon. Maybe we should make him drive out on some logging road and spend the night in whatever car he steals, then have him drive into town tomorrow morning just before work. We could give him, say, fifteen minutes at home to clean up. Then tell him to get to the bank and grab the money."

"What about the car?" asked Willie.

"Huh?"

"We can't exactly have him cruising downtown Marquette in a stolen car. What are we gonna do about that?"

"I don't know. But let's not have him go home. Let's make him sleep in it someplace in the woods. It'll be safer for us. He'll be uncomfortable and out of his element. And he won't be near a phone, so if he gets a case of the stupids he can't call the cops. *And* it'll give us time to figure out what to do about the car."

"Yeah. You're right, hon. Let's do it that way." He gave her a nervous smile. "I'm sure glad you're here. With both of us thinking this stuff through we're bound to do better. And by noon tomorrow it'll all be over." He drew a breath, then said, "We're going to have a great life, Carmen. A great life. That's all I want."

Carmen moved closer to him. Sliding her arm under his, she laid her head on his shoulder. "Me too, Willie. Me too."

Chapter 20

Geez that guy's stupid, thought Eric Kramer, as he skulked from vehicle to vehicle searching for one with the keys still in the ignition. He'd checked nearly twenty cars and pickups and was about to give up when he came upon a beat-up brown Ford F-250 three-quarter ton four-by-four with the windows rolled down and the keys dangling from the steering column. "Well I'll be damned!"

The words made both Willie and Carmen jump.

"What?" asked Willie.

"I found a pickup truck with the keys still in it."

"Well, numb-nuts, get in, start up, and drive as though your life depends on it . . . because it does."

Eric climbed in, started the truck and drove through the parking lot to the edge of 550, then stopped. "Which way?"

"Turn left and head for Big Bay," ordered Willie.

"Left it is," responded Eric. He let out the clutch, swung the wheel hard *right*, and pressed the gas pedal to the floorboard—headed in the direction of Marquette. His lips curled into a smile. *That jerk is so stupid. Even I know radio controls have a limited range. Since he wants me to go toward Big Bay it must mean he's already waiting in that direction. If I can get a few miles down the road toward Marquette I'll probably be out of range of his triggering device. And when I get to a point where I can't hear him on the radio anymore I'll know I'm safe. Then I can go straight to the police and they'll get this damn thing off me.*

"Let's get going," said Carmen.

Willie started the Ford and lurched forward toward 550 with as much speed as the overgrown trail would allow. He stopped at the edge of the highway and looked both ways. Nothing to the left. But to the right, he saw a brown pickup barreling toward them. He did a double take, then rammed the gearshift into reverse and gunned the Ford backward up the rutted road.

"I think that's Moose headed this way. Duck down so he won't see us."

Willie and Carmen hunkered down but kept their eyes above dashboard level. The brown truck was still accelerating as it passed them.

"Willie. That's not Moose!"

"I know," he said, slamming the Ford into gear. Spinning tires shrieked as they came off dirt and grabbed pavement, and Willie turned southbound in hot pursuit of his prey.

By the time he was up to speed, Eric was well out of sight. Willie pushed his truck past eighty on the straight stretches, but slowed appreciably for many of the curves. He knew the road well, and the toll of lives its curves had taken. Willie was driving for money and freedom, but Eric was driving for his life and kept Moose's three-quarter ton near eighty, even on the curves. It was only when the tail end lost traction and began drifting toward the shoulder that Eric decided dying in an auto accident wasn't any better than dying from a bomb blast—maybe worse—and slowed down. He was nearing the Harlow Lake turnoff and a thought occurred to him. Years ago his parents had purchased a satellite dish. The dish worked fine on sunny days but it was difficult to get a clear picture when it rained. Water blocks radio signals, reasoned Eric. If I can get myself into some water, that jerk can't possibly detonate the bomb. And maybe I can take my pants off and slide this thing right off of me.

The way to the lake was just ahead. Braking hard, Eric barely made the turn onto the mile-long gravel road leading to Harlow Lake. He'd traveled maybe a hundred feet when he stopped. He had to think. Was he really far enough away from the nut with the button? Would water really stop the signal? Or, would water somehow short out the circuitry and cause the damn thing to explode? Oh God! What should he do? He bent forward, head against the steering wheel. Biting his lower lip, he looked down at his sodden Dockers and ruined deck shoes. "If nothing else I'll get this damn stink off of me and die clean." Then he sat up, appraised the gravel road ahead and started off toward Harlow Lake.

Willie flew by the Harlow Lake turnoff going nearly eighty. There was a small hill coming up, after that a descending turn to the right. He'd begun braking for the turn when he heard Carmen scream, *"STOP!"*

"Willie, he's back there!" She was pointing over her shoulder. "I saw the truck. It's on the road to your place. *He's going to Harlow Lake!"*

Willie slammed on the brakes, did a cop turn and burned rubber for the turnoff. As he bounced off the pavement onto the gravel road, he entered a dissipating cloud of dust that told him Carmen was right. Eric, or someone, had just driven toward Harlow Lake. Must have been going at a good clip to raise that much dust, thought Willie. They had him now. There was only one passable road in and out of Harlow Lake. They were on it. He could follow Eric's dust trail until they caught him.

Willie knew the road like the back of his hand. He'd traveled it hundreds of times. There was no way Eric could get farther ahead of them than he already was. In all likelihood Willie would close the distance rapidly. He couldn't believe his luck. "Too bad for you, fruit cake, I'm on to you now."

And close he did. The big three-quarter ton Eric was driving couldn't take the curves nearly as fast as Willie's lighter half-ton. Before they were mid way to the lake Willie and Carmen were catching glimpses of the brown Ford. Willie slowed to the same speed as Eric. He didn't want to be spotted. He wanted to keep an eye on his prey and find out what he was up to.

Eric drove till he crossed a small wooden bridge spanning Harlow Creek. This section of the creek was the outflowage of Harlow Lake. About fifteen feet wide at its widest and barely a couple feet deep, the warm, slow-moving water of the Harlow casually wound its way northeastward, eventually passing under a bridge at County Road 550 and then on another quarter mile to empty its offering into cold, clear Lake Superior. Eric crossed the bridge, slowed, stopped, then backed up until he was on the bridge again. Good a spot as any, he thought. Pulling forward once more, he muscled the stolen truck off the gravel road into a rutted parking place used by fishermen. Turning off the engine, he climbed out of the truck, then followed a well-worn path through weedy tag alder to a narrow strip of sandy beach on the edge of the lake. After a brief period of reflection, he said, "No time like the present," and took his first step into the warm lake.

Seeing Eric stop and park, Willie pulled to the side of the road and shut off his engine. He told Carmen to stay in the truck and be ready to drive, then grabbed the control assembly and slipped out of the pickup. Abandoning the road for the cover of woods, he traveled in the general direction of the brown pickup, stopping when he had a clear view. Willie watched as Eric left Moose's truck and took the path to the lake. He didn't follow directly, but took a tangent that brought him to the shoreline a good hundred feet from where Eric stood contemplating the water. He took cover behind a thicket and gaped in amazement as Eric took his first step into the lake. What does that numbskull think he's doing? He keyed the mike on the walkie-talkie. "Go ahead!"

The voice from the speaker in the belt startled Eric, and he froze.

"Any message you want me to relay to your folks?" inquired Willie.

Eric's body remained still but his mind raced franticly. The voice from the belt had been loud and clear. He'd been wrong about the transmission range of the radio. The thought chilled him. Still he kept silent.

"Well, if there's nothing you want me to tell your next of kin, go ahead, take that next step into the water."

Without thinking, Eric took a step forward. The water was now up to his knees.

"Listen, dim-wit. There's something you should know about water."

He's here! He's right here watching me! But how? How

could he know where I am? Eric's eyes went down to the belt. Of course. There's a transmitter in the belt, and he has some way of following the signal. It could be one of those global positioning systems. This guy could probably track my position anywhere on the planet. His shoulders slumped as the precious hope he'd accrued began draining out of him into the tepid lake.

"Water is a conductor, you simpleton," continued Willie. "It conducts electricity. Get it? It's like closing a switch. It lets electrons flow. Now think. Is that what you *really* want to do? . . . let electricity start flowing in that belt? . . . I don't think so. But if you've made up your mind, *please,* don't let me stop you. I just thought I'd see if you had any last words for me to pass on to your loved ones, like maybe, 'Mom, you were right. I should have taken that science class in high school.'"

Eric didn't respond. He realized he didn't know anything at all about electricity. He'd made a guess back at the Squirrel when he turned right rather than left as instructed—thinking the *controller* couldn't follow him, that he could get out of range and be safe—but he'd been wrong. Was he wrong too about going in the water? Sadly, the answer was most likely yes. And with that realization the last of the hope seeped out of him into the tannin-stained lake. Despondent, Eric turned and shuffled back to the shore, then sat limply on the wet sand, head on his knees.

"Now," said Willie, "I think we've established a few things. Wouldn't you agree?"

"Yes," came the soft reply.

"There's no point in getting all weepy," chided Willie. "By tomorrow noon it'll all be over and your life will be back to normal. But please, till then let's be reasonable. Think about it. This is only a minor inconvenience for less than twenty-four hours. It's not worth dying over. Wouldn't you agree? Now repeat after me. It's a minor inconvenience."

Eric dutifully replied, "It's a minor inconvenience."

"It's not worth dying over," prompted Willie.

"It's not worth dying over."

"Now, why don't you sit there for a few minutes and mull that over. Better yet, why don't you take this opportunity to wash off some of that dumpster crud. You'll feel better. But while you're doing it, stay right there on the beach. And for God's sake, don't get the belt wet. Do you understand?"

"I understand," answered Eric.

Willie could hardly contain himself. He was jubilant. He was back in control. And the whole fiasco had obviously demoralized Eric. It was like one of those cult hazings where they take new recruits and put them in a strange environment and blab at them constantly and keep them hungry and tire them out until they're exhausted and confused and pliable and will do anything the Grand Poobah wants them to do. He should have thought of it sooner. But now it had worked out that way anyway, and it was important to keep it like that.

Willie slipped back through the woods to his pickup and Carmen. "It's okay," he told her. "I've got him under control again. *And* I have a plan."

He quickly explained his idea to Carmen. She listened intently, occasionally nodding agreement. Then they went to work. Willie crept back to his lookout spot on the beach and kept an eye on Eric, while Carmen, using the forest for cover, made her way to Moose's truck, removed the keys and returned to Willie's pickup.

"Okay, Eric, it's time to go."

"Go? Go where?"

"Since I can't seem to trust you with an automobile, I'm revoking your driving privileges. But don't worry, you get to go on a nice scenic walk. First I want you to go back to the truck and take everything out of your pockets. Everything. Then start hiking up the road. Don't stop till you get to where the railroad tracks cross. It's only a quarter mile or so. And Eric, let's not get cute again. Because as much as I want that money, I'm really starting to dislike you. And hastening your journey to the Great Beyond is beginning to have some appeal. So don't piss me off any more, or I'll say the hell with it and blow you up. Do you fully understand me?

"Yes," replied Eric.

"Now get going."

"Okay."

Eric started for the truck. He's right here with me, he thought. If I can just get a glimpse of him, then, at the very least, I'll know who I'm dealing with. And, if nothing else, when this thing's over I can finger the dimwit in a line-up.

As he neared the truck he felt an overwhelming urge to make another break for freedom. He can't kill me without losing his chance for the money. That's why he didn't do it when I took off the first time. Eric's courage and confidence were beginning to come back. I'll do it, he thought. As he got closer to the truck his pace quickened. Arriving, he yanked opened the door, jumped in and reached for the ignition key . . . then stopped dead. "Damn!"

"Who do you think you're dealing with, you dip-stick? Some moron? Do you think I'd trust you with a motor vehicle again after you've already demonstrated you're not a careful driver? Now put your things on the seat and start walking."

Eric's eyes scanned the woods for his nemesis, but he saw no one. There was nothing else to do, so he did what he was told. His deck shoes made squishing sounds as he slogged up the dusty gravel road toward the tracks. During the walk, he didn't think much about the bomb belt around his waist, or the possibility of death, or the ignominious prospect of being used to rob his own bank, his thoughts were coalescing around something entirely different and much, much sweeter—revenge.

I'm going to get that jerk if it's the last thing I ever do. I can try to get away between now and tomorrow when he wants me to go to the bank, or I can play it safe and get the money and give it to him. Either way, I have to get enough information out of him so the police can figure out who he is. If I take the money out of the bank and he gets away with it I'll be ruined. But, if the sleaze gets caught and the money's recovered, no one will blame me and my reputation will be unblemished.

In his normal organized manner Eric began to list what he knew about the controller: Obviously a man. Appears to be working alone, but may have accomplices. Knowledgeable about electricity. Knows who I am and that I have access to the bank. Knows this area. His knowledge is more than casual. I know this because he originally instructed me to turn left out of the parking lot of the Flat Squirrel but I turned right and, by chance, ended up here. And he's familiar with Harlow Lake, familiar enough to know there are railroad tracks ahead and exactly how far they are. He's probably local. Maybe lived here all his life, or at least long enough to have formed a detailed mental picture of the area. Do I know him? Would I recognize him if I saw him? I don't recognize the voice. The fool began by trying to use a phony voice, but now he's using his regular voice to talk to me. The accent says local, or at least from within the region. Could be from northern Wisconsin or Minnesota, but he sounds more local. How old is he? Hard to tell over the speaker, but he doesn't sound like a teenager and he doesn't sound like he's too old. Hmm . . . that's not narrowing it down much. His vocabulary and the way he uses words seems to make him, say, twenty-five to forty-five. He seems angry. Maybe I'm reading too much into it, but it appears as though he doesn't like me personally. Or perhaps it's bankers in general he doesn't like. Maybe he had some financial problems and blames them on a bank. Might even have had problems with First Northern. If he did, his customer information will still be on file. That would be a good place to start looking. Pull up a list of all of the men who've defaulted on loans, or we've had disputes with, or court proceedings against, and cull those for someone with an electronics background. I bet he'd be on that list. Then Eric's thought process was broken by the sight of the railroad tracks. "I'm at the tracks," he said.

"Good. Turn right and walk toward Big Bay."

"It's twenty miles to Big Bay," whined Eric. "I don't think I can walk that far."

"You won't have to," replied Willie. "Now get going."

Eric turned and began walking up the tracks. As he did, something new and frightening occurred to him: There's nothing between here and Big Bay except forest. If I'm not walking to Big Bay then why is he having me walk up here? Oh, no! I may have irritated him so much that he's decided to kill me. He's sending me up the tracks because he knows the line's abandoned and no one comes here. Maybe a hunter or two in the fall I suppose, but that's it. He could blow me up and the animals would pick my bones clean before anyone found the remains.

"Why are you having me walk up here?"

"Just do what I say," came the reply.

"Look. I'll do what you want. I'll get you the money."

"I know you will."

"Why are you having me walk up this way?"

"Shut your mouth and walk."

"Listen, I'm sorry for being such a problem. I was scared. I'm scared now. But from now on I'm going to do exactly what you tell me. Tomorrow morning you're going to be a rich man. Five million. I'll get five million out of the vault and bring it to you. No problem. Okay? Are we okay on this?"

"Yes."

Eric kept walking, but he'd stopped trying to gather clues. All he wanted now was to keep living. His mind was focused on the bomb belt cinched around his waist. Damn thing was so tight he didn't think he couldn't slide it down over his hips. And the latch didn't have a release on it. There didn't seem to be any way to get it off. But the controller said there was. And said he'd help get it off after he got the money. Was it true? Or was it a lie to get him to go to the bank and steal the money. Was this guy going to kill him anyway? He couldn't let him go with the belt on. The police would find a way to get it off. They'd X-ray it and their experts would figure it out. Then they'd take it apart to find fingerprints and other clues. A sound caught his attention. It was a car driving on Harlow Lake Road. He prayed it was the police coming to rescue him. But how? No one knew of his situation. Maybe someone else is driving up the road and somehow they can help me. No, it's probably the controller. Then the sound stopped. A few minutes later it started again. Eric stopped walking and listened closely. At first the sound seemed to be getting nearer, but then he realized it was getting farther and farther away. It must be the controller. He's leaving, thought Eric. Thank God! He sat down on the tracks to rest and think. He didn't say a word. He was hardly breathing. He didn't want to break the spell of the controller leaving. Oh, please, please let him be gone.

"Why are you sitting down?" The voice from the speaker shocked him. Eric leaped to his feet and began jogging up the tracks.

"Didn't I tell you to keep walking?"

"Yes, yes," he replied, slowing to a fast walk, more frightened then ever of what the controller might do.

"You know, pal," said Willie into the walkie-talkie, "criminals like you can never rest." He had a hard time saying this without laughing.

"What do you mean?"

"I mean, you shouldn't have stolen that truck. Auto theft is a major felony."

Eric was confused: What's the point? Where's he going with this? "Okay," he agreed, "I'm a criminal."

"Yeah," said Willie cheerfully, "and now you've tried to destroy the evidence."

"How did I do that?"

"Well . . . looks like you just drove ol' Moose's truck into Harlow Lake."

As soon as the words left his mouth, Willie was sorry he'd said them. What was he thinking? Why did he mention it was Moose's truck? Now Eric would know that he, Willie, *knows* it was Moose's truck. Not just *a* truck, it was *MOOSE'S* truck. He just told Eric that he knows who Moose is. Knows him well enough to know that it was *his* truck. He just gave Eric a huge piece of information about himself. "Shit-house!" cursed Willie, "Me and my big mouth." He'd been gloating about how clever he was at entangling Eric in a crime and had, for a brief, but critical, moment, been absurdly careless. So now the cops interview Moose and ask, "Say Moose, on the afternoon in question, did you happen to see anyone you know who has electronics skills?" And Moose replies, "Well now, let me think, hmm, well, no one I can think of except that guy who's always broke and pissed off and lives out by Harlow Lake and repairs electronic stuff named WILLIE SALO. Oh, Sweet Jesus! It's going to take the cops about ten seconds to figure out it was me. Shoot. I've really screwed this thing up now. Carmen was right; I shoulda kept my big mouth shut. Now what am I gonna do? Willie's self-flagellation was broken by the sound of Eric's voice.

"What do you mean? Oh, I see. You drove the truck into the lake. I get it."

"Yeah," said Willie trying to regain his composure. "After that big guy gave you a love tap you were kinda pissed so you stole a truck. Then, after you had some time to think about it you figured it wouldn't look so good on your resumé, you a bank president and all, so you tried to hide the evidence by ditching it in the lake. Too bad you left your sweaty fingerprints all over the steering wheel." As he spoke, Willie's mind raced. He'd never in his life tried so hard to think. What was he going to do now? It was bad enough he was at the bar and could be placed there by Moose and Sheila, but now that he'd mentioned Moose by name, that really connected him to the events. It would instantly make him the center of attention. This was not going to work. Things had gone wrong in a bad way. He'd been counting on anonymity. He didn't think he could withstand the intense questioning and pressure which would invariably come from this screw-up. It seemed as though there were only four choices: One, blow the doofus up right now and walk away. Two, go ahead with the plan and then, after he delivers the money, blow him up anyway. Three, go ahead with the plan and leave town fast with the money without blowing him up. The cops would be hot on his trail, but maybe he could get away. Or four, just let the dumb shit go, get rid of the belt and any other evidence, and if anyone ever asks about it, deny everything. Oh, good Lord, what should I do? Think man, *think!*

"You don't seriously think anyone's going to believe I stole that truck without being forced to, do you?"

What's going on here, Willie wondered? He's focusing on his role in stealing the truck. He doesn't seem to realize I just made a major mistake. "What do you mean Eric? You *did* steal the truck. Your fingerprints are all over it. The truck *is* in the lake. What would possibly make the cops think there was anyone else involved?"

"*You* made me steal the truck. I didn't want to steal it. *You* told me you'd blow me to pieces if I didn't. I think those are the kind of extenuating circumstances any judge and jury in the land would consider relevant."

"Oh, I get it," replied Willie. Then in a prissy, mock falsetto voice he said, "Well, officer, after that guy put the bomb on me I just had to steal the truck. You understand, don't you?"

Then using his phony bass voice, "Of course, Mr. Kramer, of course. And who exactly was it that put the bomb on you?"

Falsetto: "Oh, I'm not sure."

Bass: "And where is the bomb now?"

Falsetto: "Umm. He took it back."

Bass, "He took it back?"

Falsetto: "Yes. It was his bomb, not mine, and he wanted it back, so I gave it to him."

Bass: "Hmm!"

Falsetto: "That was the right thing to do, wasn't it? I mean, after all it was his bomb."

Bass: "Yes, Mr. Kramer. Of course."

Falsetto: "Oh, thanks so much for understanding. Because, well, I just wasn't sure you'd understand. But you're so strong and sensitive and, oh, you, you, just make me feel so safe."

Bass: "Well, Mr. Kramer, I'm afraid I'm going to have to

take you down to the station. But don't you worry, it's just routine. We'll get this whole thing straightened out in no time, no time at all. But, you understand, I'll have to read you your rights, and you'll probably want to call your lawyer just to be safe, and there's a gaggle of reporters out front who want to talk to you. Oh and, say, Mr. Kramer, did you see the headlines? BANK PRESIDENT ARRESTED FOR AUTO THEFT AND DESTRUCTION OF STOLEN PROPERTY. These are pretty serious crimes, Mr. Kramer. We're going to have to keep you in jail until Monday or Tuesday when you can have a bail hearing. But don't worry, the judge rarely throws the book at first offenders so you'll only get a couple of years. And the state pen is just south of town so all your high-class friends can stop by and visit as often as they like." Then Willie shut his mouth and waited.

Eric remained silent for a while. His analytical mind was churning through the possible outcomes. Finally, he spoke. "I have to admit, you've got a point. I've been standing here trying to think this through. And it seems, without some evidence to the contrary, the police, and more importantly the general public and my board of directors, are going to suspect I made up the part about the bomb. I'm in a tricky position here."

"I'd say," agreed Willie.

"On one hand, I'd really like to get this damn bomb off of me."

"Yes, I can certainly understand that."

"On the other hand, if you were to allow me take the belt off now and walk away, there wouldn't be any way to prove I'm not a thief."

"That's right. If I took the belt off now and vanished, your life would be a pile of horse-pucky. No one would believe you. Or, at best, there'd always be lingering doubt about your mental stability. But with the bomb, or other evidence you were coerced, you're home free. No bomb, pile of poop. Bomb, home free. See, Eric, you actually *need* me. You're much, much better off *with* the belt than without it. And you're better off going through with the plan too. Because if you do, the cops will have solid evidence that you weren't lying."

"Huh? What evidence?"

"Well, first of all, you won't have the money. Who in their right mind would steal money from their own bank, then show up at the police station and tell this story?"

"That's not enough."

"Second, I have to destroy the bomb by blowing it up. But you can bring the cops to where I've exploded it and they can see for themselves. They'll find some small fragments. Hopefully not enough to connect me, but certainly enough to convince them you weren't lying."

"So why won't they think I built it myself?"

"Eric, it doesn't make sense for you to have built the bomb. What? You made a bomb, then went to the Flat Squirrel and picked a fight with somebody, then stole a truck, then went to the bank and took a bunch of money, then blew up the bomb, then made up a story and went to the police? Come on. No way. No one's going to believe that. I'll bet you don't even know how to build a bomb. And you probably don't even have any access to explosives. Isn't that right?"

"No, of course not."

"That's right. See . . . I'm a bomber. Bombs are my life. I love bombs. I love explosives. I know lots of places to get the stuff. All kinds. You name it, I can get it. But that's not you. Money, that's your life, money and banking. So with any evidence that there was a real bomb, you're off the hook. Heck, you'll probably end up being a hero.

"Oh, come on."

"Think about it! It's going to be big news. I can see the headline now, 'Brave Banker Okay After Spending Seventeen Hours Strapped To Bomb!'"

"It's not going to seem so glamorous when they find out you put the damn thing on me when I was in a dumpster."

"Eric, Eric, no one has to know about the dumpster. Tell them I pulled a gun on you. Tell them anything you want. Make it glamorous. Make yourself out to be a hero. Heck, you might even get a promotion for this."

"Yeah, right."

"You've got to be creative."

"Creative? Bankers aren't supposed to be creative. We're not supposed to make things up. We're supposed to be efficient and practical and follow rules and regulations. No one wants a creative banker. Can't you see this is difficult for me?"

"Eric, you've got to think of your future. It's bright and shining, and it's all waiting to happen for you. All you have to do is bring me some money, then make up a little story. It's so easy. You'll probably be on the cover of *People*. Don't miss this golden opportunity. Don't screw it up for yourself. Seriously, Eric, you should sit down and think about this."

So he did. Eric sat down on a rail and thought for a full fifteen minutes while Willie watched nervously from a hiding place several hundred feet away.

At last he said, "Okay. You're right. I'm screwed without proof that somebody made me take the truck. And I'm sure you'd find a convenient way to let the police know where they can find it. I'm damned if I do and damned if I don't. But, oddly enough, it seems I'm better off being an accomplice to a robbery of my own bank than I am being a truck thief . . . so I'll do it."

Willie raised his fist in victory. "Good. You're making sense now."

"On one condition."

"What's that?"

"I want you to take this damn bomb off me so I can go home and have something to eat and get a good night's sleep—if that's possible—before I take part in this scheme." He paused for a moment, gathering his courage. "Or you might as well just blow me up right now."

Willie considered his options. "Okay."

"What?" gasped Eric, thinking he was about to be incinerated.

"Okay, I'll take the bomb off. You can go home."

Eric breathed a huge sigh of relief.

"But I have a condition too. And, strange as it may seem, this should appeal to you. Tomorrow morning you have to put the belt back on before you go to the bank. That way I'll know you'll follow through with the plan; and you'll know that if anything goes wrong, like if somehow you get stopped with the money, you'll have an out . . . because you had to do it, because you have a bomb wrapped around you."

"Let me make sure I have this straight," said Eric in disbelief. "You'll take the bomb off me now. I can go home and relax and watch TV or something, get a restful night's sleep, and then in the morning I put the bomb back on before the, ah, what do they call it in your profession? the heist?"

"Yes, Eric, that's what we call it. We never call it a robbery. That's considered passé. Peer pressure forces us to say heist."

"You don't have to be sarcastic. I wasn't trying to get personal."

"Well it sounded personal."

"It wasn't."

"Well, okay."

"You know, you were getting kind of personal too with all those names you were calling me."

"It wasn't personal. It's part of the job."

"Okay. I guess I understand. So when do we take the belt off?"

"How about right now."

"That would be fine with me. Damn thing's starting to chafe."

"Now, after we get it off, here's what I want you to do."

"What?"

"You can't be seen on 550. You've got to follow the tracks all the way into Marquette. By the time you get there it'll be dark. You need to walk all the way home. Don't let anyone see you. Do you understand? This is for your own protection as much as mine. You can't have anybody seeing you around Harlow Lake or on 550. Later, you can say that someone picked you up hitch-hiking at the Squirrel—someone who'll never be found—and drove you to your house. You can say you gave them twenty bucks or something. Then you stayed home all night and watched TV or read or something like that. Understand?"

"Do I really have to walk all the way to Marquette? It must be ten miles."

"It's only seven."

"That's a long way."

"It's not that far. It'll only take about two hours if you walk fast."

"Okay. I'll do it."

"Good. It's the smart thing."

"I suppose. But . . . ah . . . one last thing."

"What?"

"How will I get the bomb back in the morning?"

"I'll let you know."

"How?"

"That's *my* business. If I find out that you called the cops or anything like that you'll never hear from me again, and you'll never find the bomb, and you'll be screwed. I'll be watching and listening all the time, so don't mess up. Remember, you *need* this bomb. This bomb is your best friend. It's not a threat to you, it's your salvation. With it, you're a hero. Without it, you're unemployed and the laughing stock of Marquette. So how about we get to work and get that bomb off. Okay?"

"Okay."

Chapter 21

Willie told Eric to stay put for a few minutes while he made the arrangements. When everything was ready, he radioed.

"Eric."

"Yes."

"Walk back down the tracks toward Harlow Lake. About four hundred feet from where you are is a stick laying across the rail. It's on the right hand side as you're walking back. I put the key next to the stick. When you find it tell me."

"All right."

Eric walked back toward Harlow Lake and, just as Willie said, there was a stick across the track and beside it a thin key.

"I found it. Now what?"

"Listen carefully. After you open the buckle, do not let the belt drop. Do you understand? Dropping the belt could trigger the firing mechanism. You have to be very careful. Okay?"

"Believe me. I'll be careful."

"All right. Hold the key in your right hand. With your left hand turn the buckle of the belt over so you can get at the back side."

"Okay. I've done that. What next?"

"Now slide the key into the opening where the buckle goes into the latch. It's a tight fit, but it'll go. Slide it in at about the mid-point. Push it straight in."

"It won't go."

"Yes it will. But don't force it, or it could break."

"Okay, okay. I've got it in. Now what?"

"Work it upward until it won't go any more."

"It's there."

"Now gently pull on it, as if you're trying to pull it out.

Before you do, make sure you're holding onto the belt so it won't fall when it opens."

"Believe me. I'm holding the belt as tight as humanly possible. OKAY! IT'S OPEN! Oh, what a relief. As you can probably guess, I didn't really enjoy having this thing on. What should I do with it now?"

"Put it on the ground between the tracks and walk away from it. Head for Marquette like we planned, and I'll get in touch with you tomorrow. By the way, is your phone listed?"

"Yes it is. All right, I'm going. What time should I expect your call?"

"What time does the bank open?"

"Nine o'clock. We're open from nine till noon on Saturdays."

"What time do you usually get there?"

"Nine sharp."

"Be dressed and ready to leave your house by eight-thirty."

"All right."

"One last thing, Eric."

"What's that?"

"Do you want some?"

"Want some what?"

"Some money."

"No. But I'd like my wallet back."

"Sorry. No can do."

"Why? You didn't leave it in the truck did you?"

"No."

"Then why can't I have it back?"

"WALK AWAY FROM THAT BOMB YOU MORON!"

"Jesus! Yes, good point."

All the time he'd been arguing with Willie he'd been holding the belt. Now he gently set it down and began to walk away. After a couple steps he turned back and said, "Thanks. I don't know what I was thinking."

"That's what I'm here for Eric, to take care of these little details."

"Yeah, right."

"Before you go, I'll ask you once again. Do you want some money?"

"Why can't I have my wallet?"

"Don't worry about your wallet. You'll get it back to-morrow, *after* we've taken care of business. Call it an insurance policy."

"All right. But I want it back. The items in there are hard to replace."

"I know. You'll get it back. I'll put it in an envelope and mail it to you just as soon as we've taken care of business."

"Speaking of business. I'm kind of worried about my fingerprints on that truck."

"You don't need to worry about that either. The truck's in a deep spot where no one will accidentally find it. The tracks have been taken care of. After a few weeks the water will wash away your prints. And there's nothing else in there . . . right now . . . that would connect you with it. Besides, the truck will never be found."

"I get it. If I don't go along with your plan you'll swim down and put my wallet inside."

"Something like that."

"Okay."

"You still didn't answer my question. Do you want some money?"

"No. I don't imagine I'll need any between here and home."

"I don't think you understand."

It took Eric a moment before it dawned on him. "Are you talking about some of the money from tomorrow?"

"Yes."

"Judas Priest! That would make me an accomplice. I can't do that."

"Why not? Think about it. How about a cool million tucked away in a secret place no one knows about except you. You can think of it as an insurance policy, or severance pay in case something unexpected comes up at the bank. They could merge and cut costs and let you go. Or simply decide to fire you for no reason at all. Think of it as your own private 401k, untaxed and waiting to be used on anything you want; early retirement, a trip around the world, vacation home in Spain, whatever your heart desires. Why not?"

"Ahh . . . I don't know. I have a good job. They pay me well. I have a retirement plan. I really don't need the money. It's attractive, but I don't think so."

"Eric, haven't you noticed that things don't always go according to plan in life? There are changes of fortune. People suffer reversals. You must see it all the time at the bank. Don't you?"

"Um . . . yes. It's true. I do see that from time to time. But I'm secure. My job and my future are secure. I don't think it applies to me."

"Let me ask you something, Eric. Those people who had the reversals, do you think *they* ever thought it would apply to *them*?"

"Hmm . . . no, I guess not. But that's different."

"How? Things happen out of the blue. Things that are totally unanticipated. Things that can't be covered by some plan or insurance policy. Here's an example. Let's say you're walking down Front Street to the bank and a brick comes loose from the facade of one of those old buildings and bonks you on the head. And after that you're never quite the same. And the folks you work for say 'Gee, Eric, we'd like to keep you on, but, you know . . .,' and you use up all your insurance and savings, and you lose your home, and you're out in the street in the winter with no money and no job and no friends and no place to go . . . all because of some purely chance occurrence. Don't you think it would be nice to have a nest egg tucked away for just such a time?"

"That's pretty far fetched."

"It isn't. It really isn't. Why don't you just keep that in the back of your mind and give it some thought later on."

"Okay. Sure."

"One more point."

"What?"

"You could think of it as your fuck you money."

"What?"

"Fuck you money. It's so when life has you down or people are giving you a hard time you'll have enough money to say fuck you and walk away knowing they can't do a damn thing about it because you have plenty of money, enough to do anything you want."

"Umm. That's an interesting concept, but . . ."

"Sure. Think about it. I've never been a bank president but I'm smart enough to know that even bank presidents have to take crap from somebody. It's not all a bed of roses, is it?"

"No. No it isn't. It's hard work. And yes, I have to answer to others. And they're not always as ah . . . understanding as they could be."

"See what I mean. Those chowder-heads you work for could get together some day and one could say *'My little girl Agnes, you know, the ugly one with only one tit, is going out with a nice boy from Harvard, and he sure would like to be a bank president, and Agnes, she sure wants to get married and . . .'* Do you get my drift? This stuff happens all the time."

Eric thought about Annie Nancarrow. Ugh, what a bowwow. But her father was the chairman of the board, and he always had to be nice to her and go to her parties. She had the hots for him, but just thinking about her made his manhood shrivel. If she ever became angry with him and whispered in her father's ear—told some lies—he really would be looking for a new job. And it's not inconceivable if Annie were to marry someone with a banking background her father *could* move him out and the other guy in. It really *could* happen.

I must be losing it, thought Eric. This guy's starting to make sense.

"Okay," he said, "you've made some good points . . . some very good points. I'll give it plenty of serious thought tonight and let you know in the morning."

"Fair enough."

With that settled, Eric began trudging southbound along the old abandoned Marquette and Huron Mountain Railroad tracks toward the city of Marquette.

Chapter 22

It was a beautiful summer day. So nice in fact that Bob didn't even mind that he was vacuuming dried puke out of the carpet of the Cessna 152. He was wearing his "Big Where It Counts" T-shirt and singing an out-of-tune version of *Learning to Fly* by Tom Petty.

Bob Hart—Little Bob to his friends—was too short for the airlines. But he was an excellent pilot and a good all around guy. Hart Aviation, Bob's small flying service (no pun intended), had four airplanes, all of which were financed through The First Northern National Bank of Marquette: A Cessna 152 for basic flying lessons; a larger Cessna 172 RG (RG standing for the cool, retractable landing gear) for advanced lessons and sightseeing tours involving three or fewer passengers; a Citabria for aerobatic instruction (note: Citabria is airbatic spelled backwards); and the pride of his fleet, a Piper Cherokee Six, with a powerful 360 horse engine, which Bob used for larger sightseeing tours, charters and hauling parachute jumpers.

He finished cleaning the Cessna, locked the doors, secured the tie-downs and then strolled to the office to check Saturday's schedule. He noticed the local jumpmaster, Arlo Bramble, had booked himself and the Cherokee Six to haul jumpers from 11:00 to 1:00 on Saturday. Hauling jumpers was something Bob always enjoyed doing.

He left the office and walked to the hanger where the Six was parked. Opening the craft's payload doors, he removed the two rows of back seats, then loaded the parachutes Arlo always kept stored in a corner of the hanger. He'd wait till he got to Curly Field to take the doors off—less dust in the plane that way. After checking the gas and oil, and satisfied both were topped off, he locked the hanger and casually made his way back to the office to touch base with his office manager, Nan Nakashian, one last time before heading home.

"I was just about to come out and get you," said Nan as he entered the office. "Bob, this is Mr. Nancarrow." She gestured toward a short, grumpy-looking man with an expensive business suit covering a business lunch midsection. He had short-cropped, salt and pepper hair and a bulbous nose protruding from florid cheeks. "He'd like someone to fly him up to the Thunder Bay Club. What do you think?"

"One way or round trip?" inquired Bob.

"One way," replied Nancarrow. "And I need to get there as soon as possible. I was planning on renting a car to drive up, but my flight was delayed in Chicago. Now I'm running way behind. I'm expected at my daughter's for dinner. It's her birthday and I don't want to be late."

Bob didn't hesitate. "No problem. I can have you there in half an hour. With car rental paperwork and everything, that's an hour less than if you drove up."

"Fine with me," said Nancarrow. "What's the charge?"

Nan was already adding numbers in her head. One hour of flight time on the Six at one hundred thirty dollars. One hour of pilot time at fifty-five dollars. "One eighty-five," replied Nan cheerfully. "How would you like to take care of this?"

Nancarrow paid with a gold card, then grabbed his leather suitcase and walked purposefully toward the airplane Bob was already pulling out of a hanger.

Easy money, thought Bob.

Five minutes later they were in the air climbing to 2,000 feet for the short forty-mile hop to the grass strip at the Thunder Bay Club.

Chapter 23

He's pretty smart, thought Carmen as she muscled the big pickup through a curvy section of County Road 550 on her way back to the Flat Squirrel. Willie'd said to bring Moose's truck back so he doesn't get all worked up. But first, make it seem as though we drove it into Harlow Lake to get Eric thinking he's implicated in a crime. The thought made her laugh. Oh sweet freedom. I haven't had this much fun in a long time. I'd love to have that money, but just doing something, something wild, makes me feel alive again. I've missed this feeling since getting married. What a mistake. When I did it I really thought the money would be enough. I didn't realize I'd have to give up being myself. With Willie at least I can be myself. I can do and say any damn thing I please and it's okay with him. He likes me. Loves me, I guess. The real me. So, what the heck! Look out world, here I come.

Willie told Carmen to wait fifteen minutes, then drive his Ford about half way to the tracks and park it. Then to walk back to Moose's truck and drive it back to the Squirrel. If Moose didn't see her driving in, fine. If Moose did see her, she could make something up about how she was out in the parking lot, just about to leave, when his truck pulls up. The guy driving says his car ran out of gas a couple miles down 550 and he'd borrowed the truck to get back to his car with some gas, and would she come with him and drive the truck back to the Squirrel. He seemed okay, and it was Moose's truck, so she figured he must be a friend, so she says yes. After driving down to about Wetmore's Landing, the guy stops and says this is fine cause the car's off the road, by the beach, and he'll hoof it from there. He says to go ahead and drive the truck back to the Squirrel, and thanks a lot. So that's what she did.

It was kind of a lame story. But Carmen figured that Moose, even if he were upset, wouldn't for a moment think that it was her fault. After all, she had her own Jeep Cherokee right there in the parking lot. There'd be no reason on earth for her to take Moose's truck herself.

As it turned out, Carmen didn't need the story. When she turned into the Squirrel's parking lot there wasn't anyone outside. She quickly pulled into the first space available. It was way in the back. She knew the chance of it being the same spot Eric had taken the truck from was slim, but there was nothing she could do about it. She hoped Moose wouldn't notice it had been moved or, if he did notice, would be too loaded to care.

Leaving Moose's truck, Carmen hurried to her Cherokee. Surveying the parking lot to make sure everything seemed normal, she started up, drove out of the lot and motored back south on 550 toward Harlow Lake. But when she arrived at the turnoff she turned left, onto a dirt road, instead of right, toward Harlow Lake. Willie'd instructed her to go to the beach at the mouth of Harlow Creek, where it drained into Lake Superior. So that's what she did.

Chapter 24

Sam and Mattie didn't mean to cause so much trouble, they were just bored and wanted something to do. The boys, Sam—eleven, and Mathew—nine, had already built a mud dam on the small creek which flowed through their parents property and sailed stick boats in the resulting pond, pealed birch bark strips off several of the large white paper birches that grew in the woods around the rural home (the birch bark would be vital for sending secret messages back to civilization in the event of an attack by wild Indians, Nazis or space aliens), played in the tree house their father built for them, played catch, wrestled, and wandered around in the woods collecting important sticks and rocks. It was now late afternoon. School would be starting on Monday and they were desperate to extract every last ounce of joy from the few remaining hours of summer vacation. So, after several long minutes of serious contemplation they decided to indulge in some forbidden fun. But they'd have to be careful. Being the only children within a mile either way on this stretch of County Road 550, they were always the first suspects interrogated when anything out of the ordinary occurred.

Finding one of their mom's old purses in the attic, they duct taped three one-dollar bills so they were sticking half way out of the mouth and tied a forty-foot length of binders twine to the strap. Then, giggling, ran through the woods to a secret hiding spot by the side of the road. Their plan was to set the purse on the highway, then hide in the bushes watching until someone saw it and stopped to retrieve the money. They'd wait till the dupe was about ten feet from the purse, then quickly drag it off the road into the bushes. Seeing the surprised look on the victim's face was always good for a laugh. And perhaps, if the patsy became angry, for a good chase through the woods. The boys knew the area by heart: Knew every trail and hiding place. This was their turf and they were totally confident no clumsy adult would ever be able to catch them. But things didn't work out quite as planned.

The hidey spot was about a quarter mile south of the house and around a bend in 550. It had been scouted and prepared long before, purposely chosen because of its distance from their driveway. Their mother might walk to the road to check the mailbox and they wanted to be far enough away so there'd be no risk of her spying them doing something which they'd been specifically warned not to.

After untangling the twine, Sam—being the oldest and generally in charge of such things—sent Mattie out to the highway with the purse. Mattie scurried to the center of the southbound lane, dropped the bait, then ran like a felon back to their hidey place tucked away in thick bushes twenty feet off the shoulder of the road. They giggled, squirmed, talked, punched each other on the arm and slapped at the odd mosquito while waiting for some hapless motorist to cruise by. They didn't have long to wait.

Chapter 25

The Six, with its powerful engine at full throttle, climbed quickly to two thousand feet. Bob leveled off, turned to a northerly heading, eased the propeller pitch control back to the cruise setting and throttled back to 75 percent power. In moments the craft was at its normal cruise speed of 130 knots. Nancarrow was gazing out the side window in silence, watching the scenery beneath as it slid by. Ten minutes later they were over Hogsback Mountain and Bob could already see the outline of Big Bay less than twenty miles ahead. Easy money, thought Bob. Fly this guy up to the Thunder Bay Club and then head home. An extra hundred eighty-five bucks in the till without even a full hour clocked on the engine.

The Six's engine was nearing its TBO (time before overhaul point), and Bob was trying to baby it as much as possible so he wouldn't have to spend the twelve thousand for the procedure any sooner than need be. Hart Air was doing okay, but he would still have to go to the bank for a portion of the overhaul money. He'd always had a good relationship with Ken Weston, the former President of First Northern, and although he didn't know the new president, Eric Kramer, he assumed with his record of good performance on his obligations there wouldn't be any problem getting the money.

Chapter 26

Tensing with excitement, the boys saw the rust-on-brown Chevy Impala wallow round the curve. They hoped there was a man driving. Men stopped, women didn't. When the car was about 100 feet from the purse it began to slow. But, much to their disappointment, the driver, a man in his twenties with long dreadlocks, didn't stop. Laughing, he wagged his finger in the general direction of their hiding place as he accelerated away.

"Look, Mattie!" exclaimed Sam. "There's another one!"

"Geez, look at that car," said Mattie. It was an old hearse that had been brush painted purple with house paint. In it was an assorted group of teenagers from Big Bay, bored, out for a ride and looking for something to do.

"It's stopping," said Sam. "Be quiet."

Crouching in the bushes, the boys stayed completely still and watched as the car braked to a stop in the southbound lane not fifteen feet from the purse. The teens inside thought this was their lucky day. They were broke and needed gas money if they were to keep cruising into the evening. An abandoned purse with cash in it was a godsend. The driver and all six passengers piled out and ran for the purse, leaving the vehicle idling where it was. When the quickest of the bunch was about five feet from the bait, Sam gave a sharp tug on the twine and the purse hopped about a foot toward the side of the road.

"It's a trick!" yelled the driver. "Let's get 'em!" With that, the boys ran full tilt toward the purse as it slid toward the bushes. The driver was the largest and fastest of the boys. Sam saw him coming and reeled in twine as rapidly as his small arms could manage.

"Get going, Mattie!" he commanded.

Mattie didn't want to leave his big brother. In the past they'd always run together.

"Get going!" Sam shouted again. "I'll meet you at the big rock."

The nearest of the teens was within five feet now, struggling and thrashing through the saplings and weedy growth which separated the hidey spot from the road. Mattie didn't move. At last, with a final tug, Sam had the purse in his hand. The big teenager, blood rising from where a sharp branch had ripped his cheek and cursing loudly, was only a couple feet away and bearing down.

"Got it. Let's go!" cried Sam. The boys turned to run, but at the last instant a dirty hand caught Mattie by the hair.

"Gotcha," sneered the driver. "You little peckerhead, get ready for a beatin'."

Terrified, Mattie felt his bladder release and warm pee run down his leg.

"Let go of my brother" screamed Sam. "I'm the one who did it. Betcha can't catch me." With that Sam stuck his middle finger up, the way he'd seen the big kids do at school, and waved it toward the furious teen. The driver released his grip on Mattie and lunged toward Sam. But Sam was too quick for him, bolting up the trail into the woods, the angry driver right behind him and Mattie running a close third.

The boys had designed their trails well. They weaved in and out of narrow places with branches and snags that were just high enough for them to run under at full speed, but too low for anyone taller to do the same. Time and again the furious, bloody, driver would have to slow down and bend low to keep from smashing his face on branches, and each time Sam would put a little more distance between himself and the brute. About two hundred feet into the chase Mattie wisely veered off on a side trail which would eventually lead him to the big rock and Sam. Then, after chasing Sam about 800 feet into the woods, the big teen stopped. He'd lost him.

Chapter 27

Arnie Pelto was tired, but this was the last run of the day. He was hauling a full load of second growth pine logs from a cutting site near Big Bay down to Granger's Saw Mill, two miles north of Marquette on 550. He'd run through all twelve gears in the shiny black Kenworth to get the heavy load up to speed and was now cruising at the double nickel. With the exception of a curvy stretch between Sugar Loaf and Granger's, he knew he could roll nearly full speed all the way. Arnie was already looking forward to parking the rig and driving his Jimmy back up 550 to taste a couple flat ones at the Squirrel before going home. But those thoughts evaporated like sap on a hot woodstove the instant he rounded the corner and saw the purple hearse parked in the middle of the southbound lane.

"Holy Wah!"

Arnie immediately muscled the Kenworth into the northbound lane to pass the hearse, but as he did he saw a station wagon round the corner coming at him and knew in his heart that the laws of physics were stacked against him making it to the Squirrel that evening, or perhaps ever again.

Chapter 28

Doreen drove north from Wetmore's Landing and before long was passing the Flat Squirrel bar. "Welcome to the first day of your new life." She said aloud. Then laughed as she remembered another of her grandmother's sayings, "When everything's gone wrong, there's nothing left to worry about." Still smiling, she rolled her window down and enjoyed the feeling of the cool wind blowing across her face and through her hair. The previous two hours seemed more like two days. But it was over now . . . and more than likely so was her job at the bank. Well, so what! She was young, healthy, reasonably good looking and a hard worker. She'd find something. But there would be plenty of time to think about that later. Right now she was going to the Harbor Inn to have a split of Chianti and some pasta.

Rounding a curve four-point-seven miles north of the Flat Squirrel, Doreen saw, for the second time that day, her future in the shortest and bleakest of terms. Logs were scattered everywhere. It was as if Paul Bunyan was playing pick-up-sticks and had dropped a huge handful of freshly-cut, thirty-foot pines onto the middle of County Road 550. They were helter-skelter across the road and on both shoulders right up to the tree line.

Doreen rammed her foot down on the brake pedal, the brakes locked tight and the tires began an agonizing scream. Directional control gone, the Corolla immediately began a slow counterclockwise spin, rear end drifting down the crown of the pavement toward the gravel shoulder and straight toward the stump end of a huge pine. She released the brake to stop the drift and tried to steer away from the log, but as the rear end swiveled back to its normal position it didn't hold, and the Corolla did a gut-wrenching three-sixty before bashing into a log laying perpendicular to the car's direction of travel. The impact sent the blue compact airborne for twenty feet. It came down hard on its front end, the left front tire exploding from the pressure. Then the Corolla did a half turn to the right and began to roll. The last thing Doreen remembered was looking over her left shoulder, seeing a cloudless azure sky and thinking: Gee, it really *is* a nice day.

Chapter 29

"My God! Did you see that?"

Nancarrow's face was a mask of panic as he turned to Bob Hart. Bob had been scanning the sky in a 180 degree arc in front of the Six, watching for other air traffic at their altitude. He didn't expect to see any. But with the Six going 130 knots, and assuming another aircraft was headed directly at him at 130 knots, the convergence rate would be 260 knots or roughly 300 miles per hour. At that speed the two aircraft would be converging at a mile every twelve seconds. Bob knew from experience that something which, only moments before, had looked like a speck of dirt on the windshield could, short seconds later, be another aircraft on a deadly collision course. Being careless was a cardinal sin in aviation.

"What?" he asked.

"There, on the road," replied Nancarrow, jabbing a finger downward toward County Road 550. "There's an accident. Looks like a logging truck tipped over. I . . . I just saw a car spin out and roll. Good Lord! I've never seen anything like that in my life!"

The road was below and to the right of the craft. From Bob's position in the left seat of the Six he couldn't see it—except in the distance over the engine cowling. Banking sharply, he made a ninety-degree turn to the right, then leveled out and peered down at 550.

"Yeah, you're right. Looks bad. And it's around a curve. Hard to see if you're northbound."

"See the blue car?"

"Yeah, I see it."

"I saw it hit a log and flip. Is anyone getting out?"

Bob shook his head. "I don't see anyone by the car . . . or

by the truck. Must still be inside. Could be unconscious . . . or pinned in."

"Maybe we should call somebody," said Nancarrow.

Bob Hart was ahead of him. His "com" radio was tuned to Marquette Flight Service—the people that provide weather briefings and traffic advisories for pilots landing and departing. Bob turned the volume down after leaving the airport area so he wouldn't have to listen to the repetitive chatter. He now turned it up, listened to make sure no one was talking, then keyed his mike.

"Marquette Radio, Cherokee 6116 Alpha. We're about twenty north of the airport and just saw a bad accident on County Road 550, about five north of the Flat Squirrel Bar. Request you call the Sheriff's Department."

The flight service specialist responded immediately. "Cherokee one six Alpha, Marquette Flight Service. Understand you've seen an accident on 550 about five north of the Flat Squirrel. I'll call the Sheriff's Department. Do you have any other information?"

"No we don't, John," calling the specialist by name, "other than there's a logging truck that crashed and dumped its load all over the road. My passenger saw a car hit a log and flip over. We don't see any people getting out of the vehicles. They may be trapped inside."

"Roger one six Alpha. Can you do some turns over the crash site to see if you can spot anyone?"

"Affirmative. We'll stay here and take a good look. I'll radio if we see anything. But listen, the crash site is around a sharp curve in 550. Anyone coming up from Marquette is going to have a hell of a time stopping before they hit the logs or the car that's in the middle of the road. If someone's trapped inside the car it could be a real bad scene. Tell the cops they need to get here fast and close off the road."

"I read you, Bob. Marquette Radio out."

Bob had already powered back and gone into a circling descent at a medium bank using the blue car as the center of the radius of his turn. The bank allowed both he and Nancarrow to stare out the left side window at the accident site. They watched carefully, but couldn't see any movement.

Bob glanced westward at the sun hovering low on the horizon, then back downward. "It's dusk now, won't be long before dark."

"Yeah, the road's already in shadows," agreed Nancarrow. "When it gets dark the accident will be much more difficult to see for someone driving up from the south. If they come around the corner at full speed it's going to be a real mess. God help anyone who's still in that blue car." Nancarrow shook his head as if trying to erase the mental image. "Can't you buzz the road or something to get people's attention so they'll stop?"

"They'll just think we're showing off."

They both looked down at the crash site again, then Bob leveled the wings on a southerly heading, turned to Nancarrow, and said, "I think I should land the plane on that straight stretch before the curve. I can taxi to the curve and turn the plane so it's across the road for a barrier. Anyone driving up will see it with plenty of time to stop. If we don't I hate to think of what's going to happen to the next car that comes along. And if there's anyone trapped in that blue car, to them too."

"I don't know," replied Nancarrow, suddenly worried. His eyes were drawn to the thin ribbon of pavement stretching between thick stands of stout conifers. It didn't seem possible for an airplane to land in such a tight place without veering to one side or the other and slamming into the trees. He'd always felt vulnerable when flying, and never so much as during the few times he'd flown in small planes such as the one he was in. He imagined the plane crashing, himself being thrown through the windshield, eviscerated by ripped fuselage and battered to a pulp by immoveable trees. Thinking about it made his bowels loosen.

"No. There's no way you could get this plane in there without killing us. I don't want to do it."

Bob heard Nancarrow talking but his thoughts were on other things. He made his living at a dangerous occupation.

Injury or death was the price pilots paid for making mistakes. You could get away with a few, and Bob had. But he'd learned from his early errors and never made them twice. He was a careful pilot. He was responsible. He always tried to do the right thing—to put the safety of his passengers above the financial concerns of his business. If a plane needed repair he would ground the craft until the repair was done—and done right. If the weather was marginal he wouldn't let students fly—even if they complained or threatened to move to his competition. He obeyed the aviation regulations and he obeyed common sense. That, plus a measure of good luck, was the reason no one had ever had an injury while flying with him or in his planes. He was proud of his record and determined to keep it intact.

But there was more. Bob was a realist. He knew every time he took a plane up there was a chance, only a small one, but a chance nonetheless, that he would encounter a situation where a crash was unavoidable. Airplane engines are maintained to strict standards and are remarkably dependable. Yet, every year a couple of light planes go down because of engine failure. If it happens during daylight and within gliding distance of an airport, unused road or level field, that's one thing. But over a crowded city or mountains or forest or, worst of all, over water, that was another. The very worst case would be at night over water or rough terrain. If that happened there was almost no hope of survival.

Those scenarios were all bad enough, but Bob's worst nightmare was only two feet away from him. Housed in large rubber bladders inside the airplane's thin aluminum wings was nearly eighty gallons of aviation grade gasoline. It wasn't dying in a crash that scared him so much. It was thought of living through the crash and then being burned to death as gas from the ruptured bladders ignited and turned the fuselage into an inferno. It was this very thought that caused Bob to throttle back and begin his pre-landing checklist: "Mixture – Rich; Prop – Takeoff Position; Carb Heat – On; Seatbelts – Fastened. Is your seatbelt tight, Mr. Nancarrow? Make sure it's tight."

"NO!" shouted Nancarrow. "I told you I don't want to land here. It's not safe. God damn it! You can't land. I'm paying for this flight. You're working for me. Now, put your foot on the gas and get this plane up."

"Seatbelts – Fastened;" continued Bob, "Throttle – 1700 RPM; Flaps – First Notch; Downwind, 800 AGL."

"I'm telling you, Hart," Nancarrow screamed. "Get this damn thing back up. If you don't you can kiss your career good-bye. Do you hear me, Hart? Do you know who I am? I'm Raymond Nancarrow, chairman of the board of the First Northern National Bank. I'll put you out of business faster than you can take a crap. I'll make sure you lose every license you have. Now get me back to the airport. NOW!"

"Turning Base; Second Notch of Flaps; 80 knots; 500 feet AGL," and with a trace of a smile, "No traffic on the runway."

Bob Hart was terrified of being burned alive in a crash—that's why he *had* to land the plane. If someone came speeding around the corner and smashed into the overturned car there was a very good chance of a fire. And if there was anyone trapped in the blue car they were going to be burned alive. He couldn't let that happen. He wouldn't be able to forgive himself if it did and he could have prevented it.

Bob was almost certain he could land on 550 without any trouble. He'd landed on plenty of narrow runways and in far worse conditions than the ones he had today: daylight, light wind and ample runway length. The only significant problem was the pair of drainage ditches, one on either side of the road. If he veered left or right on landing, and a tire touched the gravel shoulder, the drag could pull him into the ditch. Then the plane would spin, maybe flip, and probably hit the trees. But he was a good pilot. He'd landed on worse strips than this, and in much worse weather. And that was all there was to it, he was landing.

Turning Final, he lined up with the road. "Flaps – Full; Throttle – Back; 300 feet AGL."

The ground was getting closer. It was darker now too.

His left hand made small motions with the yoke to keep the plane lined up with the dashed centerline. It appeared the county had recently repainted it and he was grateful.

Out of the corner of his eye, Bob caught Nancarrow staring at the throttle. "Don't even think—" but before the sentence was complete, Nancarrow's hand was on it. He rammed the throttle full forward, then held it with all his strength. The engine roared, and instantly the Six's nose pitched up at a sickening angle. Bob pushed forward on the yoke with all his might, but with full flaps, landing trim and full power, the nose was impossible to hold down. They were 350 feet above the ground and the Six's airspeed was rapidly slowing. In a matter of seconds the smooth stream of air flowing over the wings would burble and separate, causing the slower of the wings to drop. Then the nose of the craft would follow. They would do a gut-wrenching, low-altitude hammerhead, followed by a steep spiral. A death spiral. At three hundred fifty feet above the ground there would be no time to recover. They would augur into the pavement at over a 100 miles per hour. Bob was in a rage of anger and panic. With his upper torso pressed hard against the yoke, he balled his right fist and swung back-hand, giving it everything he had, and caught Nancarrow flush on the nose. Nancarrow howled as blood spurted from his nostrils, but he didn't release the throttle.

That's it, thought Bob. We're dead.

Time seemed to stand still for him as the plane—struggling for altitude, engine screaming—hung on the brink of a stall. Bits and pieces of his life flashed thought his mind: His parents; his friends; his childhood in Mar-quette; the beauty of life itself; the girls he'd dated; of join-ing the Mile High Club with Susan Collens in the back of the Six; of that crazy time with Arlo and Dave when Arlo shut off the engine and jumped out with the key and Dave had to dead stick the plane back . . . *THAT'S IT!* Little Bob freed his left hand, grabbed the ignition key and turned off the ignition. Then switched hands on the yoke and used his right hand to pull the gasoline mixture control to the FULL

OFF position. Immediately the engine began to rev down. Within seconds it had stopped.

Nancarrow, realizing what had happened, was insane with fear. He started swinging and scratching at Bob, screaming, "Keys! Give me the keys!"

"You want 'em?" taunted Bob. "You get 'em." And with that, he tossed the keys over his shoulder, deep into the cargo hold of the Six.

Nancarrow clawed his seatbelt till it released, then launched himself back between the seats into the cargo area, eyes wild, searching for the life saving keys. With Nancarrow no longer a threat and the engine off, Bob pushed the nose of the craft down and with enormous relief watched the airspeed indicator begin to climb. Then he pulled off one notch of flaps to reduce the drag, oriented himself with the road and began a bank to realign himself with the centerline of 550.

The struggle with Nancarrow had eaten up more than half the landing distance. The problem now was not too little altitude, but too much—too high to land and too low to glide around and for another try. Bob pulled the third notch of flaps back on. The craft slowed and descended more rapidly, but he knew it wasn't enough. Then he twisted the yoke right and simultaneously kicked in full left rudder. The plane went into a hard crab—turning thirty degrees sideways to the direction of travel. With the entire fuselage acting as an airbrake the plane slowed dramatically, seemingly dropping from the sky, and Bob pitched the nose downward to compensate for the loss in airspeed. The ground was now rapidly approaching. Just before the wheels touched the pavement Bob released both rudder and aileron, the tail whipped back into its normal position, and plane straightened out. Then he flared the craft, bringing its nose upward to expose more wing surface to the air, and made a textbook landing on the centerline of County Road 550.

Once the nose wheel made contact with the asphalt Bob applied as much of the brakes as he dared without locking the wheels. The straightaway was gone, but he continued to brake hard while turning with the curve. He was approaching the accident scene. It would be close. The plane finally stopped rolling with the prop hanging above the first log.

"Watch your step as you exit the craft," said Little Bob to no one in particular.

Chapter 30

Carmen parked the Jeep and walked to edge of the jack pines, stopping where the sand sloped to meet the warm, slow-moving water of the Harlow as it traveled its last hundred yards before emptying into Lake Superior. Like most sandy-bottomed rivers, the Harlow didn't run straight into the big lake. Coming within fifty feet of its destination it made a right turn with the direction of the prevailing wind, then traveled parallel to the shoreline for a while before succumbing to the inevitable and turning to meet Superior and present its offering.

She sat on a soft duff of brown and gold pine needles, lit a cigarette and gazed out over the Harlow to the white sugar-sand beach that formed the spit between river and lake. Tall clumps of marram grass swayed in a barely perceptible breeze. A covey of pipers wandered about, randomly pecking for dinner near the water's edge. A lone white gull was flying off shore.

She was stubbing her cigarette when Willie arrived. She hadn't expected him so soon. She asked what happened and he told her. When he got to the part about taking the belt off Eric and letting him go, she sat bolt upright.

"What! You let him go? Do you seriously think he won't go to the police? Do you seriously think he's going to wake up tomorrow morning and say to himself, 'Hmm, nice day. Guess I'll get dressed, eat breakfast, brush my teeth and, oh yeah, put on that bomb belt and get to work. Better hurry 'cause I don't want to be late.'"

Willie explained again about his slip of the tongue regarding Moose's truck, and tried to reassure her that Eric was worried about his reputation and his ability to avoid prosecution for stealing it. He tried to convince her that if they could bind Eric tightly enough to some crimes, then they would really have him. And if they had *him*, they had the money. Then he told her about offering Eric part of the money. Carmen gaped at him as though he'd lost his mind.

"He'll never do it," she said emphatically.

"It's possible."

"No way."

"Way, Carmen. Everyone wants it. Everyone wants to have a big stash of cash, right now, easy, no fuss, no muss. Everyone. Even mister bank president. Don't you think when he's in there every day checking out all that green the thought of breaking off a chunk for himself doesn't occur? But he can't. He's trained not to. He doesn't even try to think up a plan to get it because it goes against everything he's been taught to do. But now here we come with a plan where he can get himself a major chunk of change with absolutely no blame at all. I'd be willing to bet he's thinking about it right now."

"I think you've been spending too much time alone in your cabin."

"Carmen, wait. Listen. What's he gonna do? There's no way he can prove we made him steal Moose's truck. What's he gonna say? 'Those nasty people with the bomb made me do it?' No way. Since he doesn't have the bomb, that's not gonna wash."

"But letting him go, geez Willie, are you sure that was a good idea?"

"No, I'm not sure. But what's done is done and we have to move on. So here's what I think we should do. Eric started walking toward Marquette about fifteen minutes ago. If he does what I told him, he should be there in about an hour and forty-five minutes. I want you to drive to where the tracks lead into Marquette and watch for him and make sure he really did it and didn't double back or something else. If he does the hard thing, which is to walk the seven miles all the way into town, then he's at least somewhat hooked into the plan. If he does the easy thing, doubles back and walks out on Harlow Road, then he's definitely *not* hooked into the plan. Either way, we'll pretty much know.

Well . . . we won't know for sure, but at least we'll have an indication. What do you think?"

"Um, I guess so. But what if he walks out on Harlow Road?"

"That's a tough one. But I'd say just hide the belt and lay low. He's obviously not in sync with the plan and he's probably gonna call the cops. I mean, if I had a gun I could make him put the belt back on. But I don't have a gun, and I don't really like that kind of confrontational stuff. Anyway, then he'd see me and might recognize me, or at least be able to identify me later on, and that would mess everything up. So I don't want to do it unless I have to. So, I suppose if he doesn't go along with the plan, the best thing to do is to lay low. Then in about a week or so, grab the son of a bitch some morning before the bank opens, slap the belt back on and tell him 'It's money-time banker boy or you're toast,' and mean it."

"Okay, well, at least that puts my mind at ease about one thing. You're not giving up."

"Giving up? Hell no. That's my money. Our money. He's got it. I want it. And I'm gonna get it. I've got a taste of this thing now. I've already started to live the life. I can't see myself going back to where I was before. It's time to move on. To move up. I'm not gettin' any younger. And there's a world out there that's waiting for us. There are things to do. Places to go. Good times to have. No babe. No way. I'm not giving up. Hell no! I haven't even started yet. Now come on, we've got work to do. One day of work ahead of us, then we retire."

"I'm with you, Willie. All the way."

"I love you, Carmen. I always have. Let's do this thing and do it right, then live the life."

Carmen wrapped her arms around him and kissed him hard on the mouth. When it was over she said, "Okay. So I watch to see if he comes out in Marquette. Then what? Follow him home?"

"Yeah. Watch for awhile to see if you can get some indication of what he's doing. Then meet me at ah . . ."

"Why don't we meet at my place? Dick's gone. I'll fix us something to eat and we can plan what to do next."

"Yeah, okay. I guess so. Seems kind of strange. You sure he's not going to show up?"

"He's in Minneapolis. Left this morning. Won't be back till Sunday night at the earliest."

"All right. I'll see you there in a couple hours. But right now you'd better take off for Marquette. And you might want to be seen shopping or something before you start your lookout. An alibi may come in handy later if the worst should happen. I'm gonna to go up to Big Bay and be seen having a drink there. I was drinking at the Squirrel and then went up to Big Bay to have a few. That's believable, don't you think?"

"Oh, I think anyone who knows you would say it's be-lievable."

"Ah . . . yeah."

"My place in three hours. See you there."

Carmen kissed Willie again and then drove off in the Jeep toward Marquette.

Willie watched her go. Then he stood there for awhile thinking about how involved Carmen had become in his plan. It surprised him. She had it made with Dickey. But she was willing to give it all up to do this with him. Was it only the money? She'd almost certainly married Dickey for the money—as much as told him so earlier at the Squirrel. Yes, for sure Carmen wanted the money, but it was more than that, they had something special. And it was more than great sex, it was the conversation too, and the easy familiarity— they had fun together, they were pals. The only reason she'd left him in the first place was for the money. He could un-derstand that. And if *he* had money, if *they* had money, then there wouldn't ever be any reason to leave. He wasn't sure how long he and Carmen would last, but he knew he wanted to find out, and the first step in finding out was to get mov-ing and get the money.

Willie climbed into the Ford and headed for Big Bay.

Chapter 31

The door of the Cherokee Six swung open and Bob climbed out. Then he unlatched one of the cargo doors to let Nancarrow out. Nancarrow was furious. His nose was swelling and there was blood spattered on the front of his shirt.

Looking him directly in the eye, Bob said, "The only thing hurts worse than a punch in the nose is getting hit there a second time." Nancarrow instinctively put up his hands to protect his face and moved back a step.

"We've got work to do, Mr. Nancarrow, and you're going to help me. Am I making myself clear?"

Nancarrow nodded.

"We have to turn the plane and get it back around the curve so people can see it. If we don't, the next car that comes cruising round the corner is going smash into it. Understand?"

Nancarrow nodded again.

"You can think what you want of me, and you can do whatever you think you have to *after* we take care of this situation. Is that clear?"

Nancarrow nodded some more.

"Okay. Did you find the keys?"

"No," relied Nancarrow.

Bob glanced at the pile of chutes and miscellany in the cargo hold, took a quick mental inventory of the dozens of places where the key could be hiding, then said, "We need to push the craft."

Bob closed the doors, then, under his direction, they moved the plane backward, away from the log, by pushing on the leading edge of the tail wing. They continued pushing until the plane was about a hundred and fifty feet back up the road from where it had stopped. It was now right at the end of the straight stretch before the curve. Then, pushing down on the tail, they lifted the nose wheel off the ground and swiveled the aircraft ninety degrees, making an effective visual and physical blockade to guard the accident scene.

As soon as the plane was turned, Bob said, "You check the truck. I'll check the car."

Pushing the plane, and mostly just having his feet safely back on the ground, had restored some of Nancarrow's normal thinking, so when Bob said, "Check the truck," Nancarrow replied, "Got it," and took off at a run toward the overturned Kenworth. Bob was running too, running for all he was worth toward the blue Corolla, and the woman he saw trapped inside.

Chapter 32

He raced toward the overturned car as fast as his legs would take him. There were logs and broken glass everywhere. As he closed to within thirty feet the hair stood up on the back of his neck. *Gas! I smell gas.* As he moved closer the odor was nearly overwhelming. The pavement around the car was glistening with it, and fear made him stop short.

He forced himself to stay focused on the overturned car. In it was a woman hanging upside down by her seatbelt. Her arms dangled loosely, hands and forearms resting on the flattened top. She had dark brown hair and an attractive face which would have been more attractive if her mouth weren't hanging open. He couldn't see any movement and wasn't sure if she was dead or simply unconscious. "Oh, God! Don't let her be dead." Young and beautiful, in the prime of life. Probably on her way home from work or out to visit friends. Comes around a corner and then this. "It's not fair," he said. Then, gathering his courage, he stepped into the expanding ring of gasoline and carefully made his way to the driver's side door.

Bending low, Bob studied the woman's face. She wasn't moving and he couldn't tell if she was still alive. "Miss?" he said gently. "Miss?" No response. He said it again but louder. Still no response. With one hand braced on the side of the car for balance, he reached in with the other and held his palm in front of her mouth. He could feel her breathing. She was alive! Out of relief, and because he couldn't think of anything else to do, he stroked her cheek with his fingers.

"Doreen, it's time to wake up! You're going to be late for school honey!"

She could hear her mother's voice. But she was tired and didn't want to wake up. No, Mom, she thought, just a little longer, and tried to keep sleeping. But her mother kept talking. "You need to get up, darling. Wash your face and then come on down and have your breakfast. I poured some milk on your cereal for you already, sweetheart. It's Rice Crispies. Just what you like. Come on, honey, don't let them get soggy. Gotta get going, baby or I'm going to be late for work. Doreen, wake up. Can't miss school. Doreen, please wake up, can't miss school, can't miss, miss, miss, miss, wake up, miss, please, wake up, wake up now."

"What?" Her mom's voice was changing—getting deeper. Doreen thought she should remind her mom to take her estrogen pills before she began having problems with hair growth. She could feel her mother's fingers rubbing her cheek and began to wonder why her mom would strap her upside down in a sitting position in her bed? She thought it must be one of those motorized adjustable beds she'd seen advertised for old people late at night on the boring channels. The couples in the commercials always seemed so happy. She wondered how they could be happy being seen on TV in their pajamas? And wouldn't that smiling woman be happier if the old codger lying next to her would stop fiddling with the remote control? She remembered what Willie'd said about television, "Watching TV is like living life second hand." Actually he'd used more colorful language, but she'd cleaned it up before storing it in her memory. Everything was sex to him. If only she could meet a normal man, not one who thought underwear was invented to keep his brain warm. Why can't men think about anything except . . . Huh? Oh! There was her mom calling her again, All right, mom, I'll get up, she thought. And Doreen slowly opened her eyes. Her bedroom had changed! And her mom's voice was so much deeper than it used to be. It almost sounded like a man. A man? It *is* a man! What's a man doing in my bedroom?

Then the events of the previous half hour began to come into focus. She realized she was in her car, and that her car must be upside down, and that some man was trying to wake her up, trying to help her, a good man trying to help. Well . . . she'd wanted to meet someone new. Someone who didn't think like Willie. Maybe fate was on her side. She turned her head and tried to focus on his face. He was good-looking, with caramel-brown hair combed straight back, hazel eyes and a strong squared-off jaw framing a friendly smile. And he cared enough to stop and help. The man had stopped talking—most likely because he could see she was awake. She felt she should say something, but couldn't quite think of what a person in this situation should say. So she said the first thing that came to mind. "Nice day." The words came out slow and slurred.

"Yes," replied Bob, "it sure is." And he meant it. Then tentatively, "Are you okay?"

"I think so. I hurt a little. But I don't think anything's broken."

"We'd better get you out of here. Can you undo your seatbelt? I can help keep you from falling when you unbuckle. If you brace yourself on the roof you can swing your legs down and crawl out."

"Okay." Then a moment later, "I can't get the buckle loose."

"If you don't mind me reaching around you, I might be able to do it."

Doreen replied, "I don't mind." And actually smiled a little when she said it.

Bob realized he'd have to lie down on the pavement and scoot his body partway into the car to reach the buckle. He was keenly aware that his pants and T-shirt would then be sopping up gasoline.

"There's a lot of spilled gas," he cautioned, "so we have to be careful about sparks. Is the ignition off?"

Doreen looked. "No."

He'd figured as much. Bob tried to think if it would be better to leave it where it was and hope there was nothing that could arc and ignite the fuel, or turn the key off and risk having that action itself cause a spark. In the end he reasoned it would be better to leave well enough alone, get the woman out as fast as possible and get away from the car.

Fear knotted his stomach as he lay on his back on the

wet pavement. Instantly he felt the chill of gasoline as it wicked through his shirt and pants to his skin. It was his worst nightmare in progress and he was terrified. Sweat ran into his eyes as he used his hands and forearms on the gassy asphalt to push his upper body into the vehicle.

Doreen watched as Bob's head inched into the car. He really is a handsome man, she thought. As he moved farther in and she saw the writing on his T-shirt she silently added, but they're all the same.

"Ready," he asked?

She braced her right hand and forearm against the roof of the overturned car and held onto the steering wheel with the other. "Ready as I'll ever be."

Bob pushed hard on the latch and it popped open. Immediately, Doreen fell straight down and Bob instinctively reached up to keep her from falling on him. He had his hand on her thigh and the extra pressure stopped her fall.

Doreen felt his hand holding her and couldn't resist saying, "Well okay. But no further than this on the first date."

The comment momentarily broke Bob's fixation on the gasoline and he smiled. "Okay."

Doreen was able to do a half cartwheel into a crawling position with her knees on the passenger side interior ceiling of the Corolla. Once she was down, Bob began pulling himself out of the vehicle. After he was out he helped Doreen crawl out, bunching her dress around her thighs so it wouldn't drag in the gas. Then, helping her to her feet, they quickly moved away from the car and the circle of spilled fuel.

Once they were a safe distance from the Corolla Bob relaxed, letting out a sigh. "Whew! I hate being that close to gasoline."

It was only then that the full impact of Doreen's previous situation dawned on her. One tiny spark and she would have been engulfed in flames and burned to death. The thought made her weak, she grabbed Bob's arm for support. The arm was wet. Then she looked at him and realized the man standing next to her was completely soaked—soaked with gasoline! He'd crawled on his back in a pool of gasoline to save her, knowing all along the slightest spark would mean a horrible death. And he did it for her, a total stranger. He was the bravest person she'd ever met. Probably the bravest person in the world. Turning to face him, she took hold of his hands and gazed into his eyes as tears rolled down her cheeks.

Chapter 33

Arnie heard the airplane land and the men arguing. One came up to the cab, looked in, saw him lying there and asked if he was hurt. He told him the truck went on its side, skidded off the road, then stopped when it hit the trees. He hadn't been wearing a seatbelt and the impact of the stop rammed the steering wheel into his mid-section. He told Nancarrow he thought there was something messed up inside because it was hurting bad. Then, almost as an afterthought, said his leg was broken.

Nancarrow didn't know what to do. Under the best of circumstances Arnie would have been too heavy for him to lift, and he certainly couldn't pull him up and out of the tipped over Kenworth. "I need to get help. I'll be right back."

Nancarrow walked back to where Bob was standing—noting he'd gotten the woman out of the blue care, and that she was holding his hands and gazing at him like he was a saint. Nancarrow explained about the man in the truck and Bob rushed to the Kenworth to see for himself. Bob spoke to Arnie and told him everything was going to be okay. Then, after appraising the situation, decided the best course of action was to break the windshield and pull him out. With Arnie's broken leg and the pain in his abdomen there was no other way.

Arnie said there were tools in a box attached to the side of the truck that was facing the sky. As Bob clambered up to get them, Nancarrow fetched a blanket from the airplane. When all was ready, Arnie pulled it over his face. Then Bob used a tire-billy to smash out the Kenworth's windshield. He'd stripped off the sodden T-shirt, and Doreen watched rapt as the muscles in his back, shoulders and arms rippled as he worked.

Clearing away as much of the broken glass as possible,

Bob, Doreen and Nancarrow helped Arnie crawl out through the hole where the windshield had been. The ground in front was a flat and thick with switchgrass. They lay the injured driver there and tried to make him comfortable. His breathing was shallow and rapid. It was clear he was in great pain.

While they were attending to Arnie a woman hurried toward them on the shoulder of the road from the direction of Big Bay. Reaching the group, she told them her boys said they heard a crash. Said she'd walked down the straight stretch from her house and started around the curve, saw the mess and ran back to her house to call the Sheriff's Department. She told the boys to stay put and came back to see if she could help.

"Yes, ma'am," said Bob, "you could go back and call the Sheriff's Department again and say there's a man injured and we need an ambulance immediately." She nodded and turned to go. "And if you have a car or truck or something, park it across the road so no one driving down from Big Bay smashes into this." Gesturing toward the logs and vehicle in the road. She explained her husband had taken their car to work but she had a bright yellow Case backhoe parked in the backyard, and she knew how to drive it. Then she hurried away.

A few minuets later a Sheriff's Deputy arrived. He told them he'd been at the Flat Squirrel taking a report on a stolen truck that didn't seem to be stolen after all, when some kids in an old hearse tore in saying there'd been an accident.

He asked everyone for their name and what they knew about the mishap, writing the information on a small pad.

"Not much we can do till the ambulance arrives. Should be here in about forty-five minutes or so. I'll put in another call to make double sure it's on the way, then I'd better get out there." Nodding his head toward the road. "Make sure none of the happy-hour crowd from the Squirrel rams your airplane."

Chapter 34

As Willie passed the Squirrel he glanced at his watch. An hour and a half had gone by since he'd been there with Carmen, sitting in the truck, telling her his plan. It had been the most intense hour and a half of his life and he loved it. It had been an emotional roller coaster of the *n'th* magnitude, with highs so high that sex couldn't touch it, and lows so low drugs wouldn't help. He had a big dream working. And the big dream had a big payoff. And each moment within the structure of the dream was like a perfect day. And each action he took to make the dream continue added strength and beauty to the fabric of it. And when the money was in his hands, the fabric of the dream would be complete, and the dream would merge with reality.

He'd been so frightened and then felt so powerful. He thought it must be nearly the same feeling as playing poker for a million dollars and being dealt a royal flush. Then trying to protect your winnings in a gunfight, but you run out of bullets. And at the very same time you find out that the most beautiful woman in the world wants to have your baby. But there's a lynch mob converging on you from all sides. And your feet have been glued to the floor. But an earthquake breaks apart the boards. And you realize you're standing next to a helicopter, and somehow you know how to fly. But it runs out of gas over the ocean. You fall a thousand feet to the surface, but land softly and never get wet, because you've learned to walk on water.

"Oh yeah. I'm wearin my Jesus shoes. Gonna walk on water. Gonna ride a rainbow. I'm gonna . . . *Holy Mother!*"

As Willie came around a bend four miles north of the Squirrel he thought he might be hallucinating. In the distance were colors—reds and blues—and they were flashing.

Then his body tensed and his mouth went dry. Fear and desperation were all he knew. It was a roadblock . . . they had him . . . but how? How could Eric have gotten to a phone so quickly? How could the cops have gotten up here so fast? The Sheriff's Department is in Marquette. It wasn't possible. Was it? Unless they'd been up here for some other reason and gotten the call. *"Attention all cars. Attention all cars. Mad bomber heading north on 550. Considered armed and dangerous. Just shoot the fucker".*

A quarter mile ahead of him was a line of cars moving slowly toward a police cruiser parked across the road with its lights flashing. Willie immediately slowed, thinking it might be best to turn and run. But he knew if the cruiser gave chase it would only be a matter of a minute or two before he was overtaken. What then? What could he do? He dropped the gearshift down into first and crept forward, reasoning that movement toward the cruiser would give him more time to think. He saw the car closest to the cruiser pull off to the right shoulder, then make a one-hundred-eighty-degree turn and accelerate in his direction. Was it a cop? It couldn't be a cop because he didn't think even undercover cops drove rusty Volkswagens. The next car did the same. The cop wasn't stopping them. He wasn't checking them. He was turning them around. Why? Don't they usually let people through roadblocks if they're not wanted for anything? It didn't seem right to not let people through to their homes in Big Bay. Willie's window was open; as the Volkswagen came near he waved his arm to flag it down. Two boys, about eighteen, looking like they were on their way to a Friday night party, slowed, then stopped.

"What's going on up there?"

"There's an airplane on the road," answered the driver. "I guess there was an accident up around the corner. Logs all over the place. Can't get through. If you want to get to Big Bay you have to go back to Marquette, then take US-41 toward Negaunee and catch 510. That's what the cop told us."

Willie's panic meter came off red-line and he allowed his autonomic nervous system to resume control of his breathing, then he nodded and waived. The driver put the beetle into gear and chugged away.

If it's an accident then it's not about me, he thought with relief. I couldn't figure how they'd get here so soon anyway. Still, there's a chance they're looking for me. Should I turn around here and maybe arouse suspicion? Or should I try to act like everyone else and risk getting too close? Wait a second! I came up here to establish an alibi. What better alibi is there than having talked to a cop? It's risky, but it's the best damn alibi possible. If someone did something wrong, the last person on earth they'd stop and talk to would be a cop. So that's exactly what I should do. I should stop and talk to the cops.

Willie marshaled his courage and drove forward. As he got closer he could see the airplane parked across 550 right before the corner, but he couldn't see any logs or vehicles.

Entering the short line of cars at the blockade, he could see there was only one cop. It seemed everyone was asking the usual gawker type questions: What happened? Why did the plane land? Is anybody hurt? Willie figured he should too, so when it was his turn at the front of the line he inquired, "Accident ahead officer?"

"Yeah. Logging truck tipped over and spilled its load. Car rammed into the logs. It's a mess."

"Don't suppose there's any way I can get through to Big Bay?"

"Sorry. Roads impassable."

"What's the deal with the airplane?"

"Some people were flying to the Thunder Bay Club and saw the car hit the logs and flip. Pilot landed on the road and they pulled a woman out of the car."

"Who is she?" asked Willie trying to prolong the conversation.

"Some woman from Marquette," said the deputy. "Why do you ask?"

"Ah . . . I was supposed to meet my girlfriend up in Big Bay tonight," he lied.

"What's her name?" asked the cop.

Willie's mind went blank. Then he almost blurted out, "Oh, Carmen Hodges. You know, Dickey Hodges wife." But thought better of it and said, "Doreen."

The cop's face morphed from detachment to interest. He moved in closer. The change in proximity made Willie extremely uncomfortable.

The cop asked: "What kind of car was she driving?"

"It's a Corolla. A blue Corolla."

The deputy moved even closer, looking directly into Willie's eyes, and asked, "What's your name?"

Geez, what have I done now? I've got a bad feeling about this. This guy's *way* too interested in me. Maybe he *did* get a radio call but didn't pay much attention to it—till now. Willie hesitated far too long, then finally mumbled, "Willie . . . Willie Salo."

"Mr. Salo, you'd better pull around the cruiser and park on the other side."

Willie's heart stopped pumping, but there was enough blood left in his brain to ask, "Why? Have I done something?"

"Mr. Salo, I think your girlfriend was in that car."

Willie was confused. "What car?"

The cop thought Willie might be retarded so he said the words slowly, "Mr. Salo, the car that hit those logs and overturned is a blue Toyota Corolla," giving strong emphasis to the words *blue* and *Toyota Corolla*.

Willie was dumbfounded. The last time he'd thought about Doreen was mid-afternoon when he called to see if she wanted to come out to his cabin to play hide-the-salami. Now she's been in an accident? And he'd just told this cop that he was going to Big Bay to meet her? Well, I guess he's going to remember me now, he thought. And probably find out I lied to him too. I really need to take Carmen's advice and keep my mouth shut.

The Sheriff's Deputy saw Willie's expression and thought to himself: I'll never get used to seeing the pain on a person's face when they find out a loved one's been injured.

"Mr. Salo, you can drive around the cruiser and park. But you'll have to walk from there."

"Ah . . . thanks officer. I'll do that."

Willie pulled around the cruiser and parked. He was faced with a quandary. He really did want to see if Doreen was okay. It wasn't that she didn't matter. It's just that over past couple of hours everything had changed and he'd completely forgotten about her. Doreen? Doreen who? It was Carmen now. Carmen was back in his life. When he thought of a woman, the only image that came into focus was Carmen. It would seem strange, almost obscene, to walk up to Doreen, who may be in God knows what condition, and say the kind of nice things, the kind of comforting things that an injured woman who was, until this afternoon when she told him to get lost, his girlfriend, of sorts. Willie shook his head. Life sure throws you some funny curveballs.

He got out of the truck and started walking at a pace he felt was fast enough to be appropriate but no faster. He didn't want to arrive at where Doreen was before he could think of something to say that didn't sound idiotic, like "Say Doreen, I know you dumped me this afternoon and it's pretty clear you've been in a real bad accident, but I thought if you weren't too banged up you might want to come over to my place later and . . ."

"Oh yes, Willie, thanks for being so sensitive, I'd love to come over and ride the bony pony tonight. Just let me duct tape my leg back on and we'll go."

Sure.

He'd walked about fifty feet when he froze in mid-step and almost fell forward. Steadying himself, he turned his head and stared back at the pickup. It was parked less than twenty feet from the police cruiser. The doors were unlocked. The driver's side window was rolled down. Behind the front seat, under an old gray towel, was the bomb.

Oooh, damn! What if there isn't any traffic and the cop starts nosing around my truck? What if he rummages around behind the seat to see if there are any open containers or anything? What can I do? I can't stop and go back. He's sure to get suspicious. Oh yes, officer, I forgot to roll up my window and lock the doors. You know how pesky those mosquitoes can be. Don't want the darned things getting inside while I'm checking to see if my loved one's been dismembered. And about the doors, ah, well, one can never be too careful now, can one?

There was nothing to do except keep walking, get over there as fast as possible, say the right words to Doreen, then get gone at the speed of light.

Chapter 35

Willie passed the airplane and inspected the wreckage that lay ahead: logs everywhere, Doreen's car upside down in the middle of the road and a logging truck on its side against the trees. He saw Doreen, near the truck, kneeling next to a man lying on the ground. There was another man with no shirt standing next to her, and a third sitting on a log some distance away.

"Say, Doreen, I think your car's going to need a little touch-up," quipped Willie as he approached the group, incorrectly thinking humor was appropriate auto accident etiquette.

"Thanks for asking, Willie, I'm fine." Then her face scrunched in puzzlement, "What are you doing here?"

"I was at the Squirrel and got bored so I thought I'd head up to Big Bay and watch the sap run. You?"

"It's a long story."

Doreen turned to Arnie Pelto who'd begun to moan. "Arnie . . . Arnie . . . ," she said gently, "it won't be much longer. The ambulance will be here soon. Everything's going to be okay." But Doreen was beginning to think it wasn't going to be okay. When the men helped Arnie out of the truck he'd seemed in pain but clear-eyed and lucid. But now he didn't even try to respond when she spoke to him, and he had a tired and distant look in his eyes. Doreen sensed she was watching him die.

"This isn't going to work," she said looking up at Bob. "We've got to do something. We've got to get him a hospital *now*. There's something wrong inside of him and if we wait for an ambulance and he takes that long curvy ride back to Marquette, I'm afraid . . . well, I'm just afraid."

"I could fly him back," said Bob. "The air's calm and it'd be a gentle flight. We could be at the airport in fifteen minutes. The hospital isn't far away. If the Deputy put in a call now they could have an ambulance standing by when we land."

"Let's do it. Let's not wait. Let's go now."

"All right," said Bob, then paused to think. "We have to push the plane back as close as we can to the logs so we won't have to carry him very far. We'll need as many people as possible to help carry him. He must weigh two-twenty or better so it's not going to be easy. And we'll need the deputy to move his cruiser and set up a roadblock at the far end of the straight stretch.

Willie broke in. "I'll go tell the deputy what's going on. My truck's up there and I have to move it anyway. And I'll round up some guys to help carry him."

"Run, Willie," urged Doreen. "Every second counts."

"I'm on it, hon." He turned and jogged away.

"Mr. Nancarrow," yelled Bob.

"What?" barked Nancarrow. He'd wandered away from the group after helping extract the driver from the cab of the logging truck, and sat on a log, alone, stewing in his own juices. He was as angry as he'd ever been. Angry because he wasn't at his daughter's house having dinner, because the jackass pilot had punched him in the nose, then landed against his wishes, then ordered around like a servant. Him. Raymond Nancarrow. Just who did the jerk think he was dealing with? Come tomorrow he'd sure as hell find out.

Bob ran to where Nancarrow was sitting. "The truck driver's in bad shape and getting worse by the minute. We've got to get him to the hospital. I'm going to fly him back to town. I need your help to push the plane back so we can get him on board."

Nancarrow's eyebrows went up. "Oh no you're not," he fumed. "You're going to leave that airplane right where it is so the federal aviation people can see what you've done. That guy's going to be all right. You only want to fly your plane out of here so it won't be impounded. But I'm not going to let you do it. You're going to lose your license for this Hart. I'll see to that."

Bob pleaded and then threatened but to no avail, Nancarrow was beyond it all. Bob wanted to grab him and pound on his face for a while to see if he'd change his mind, but thought better of it and ran back to where Doreen knelt caring for the driver.

"Doreen . . . . It's Doreen isn't it?"

"Yes?"

"I need you're help. It takes two people pushing down on the tail of the airplane to lift the front wheel off the ground so the plane can be turned around. Do you feel up to it?"

"Sure. But what about him?" She cast a glance at Nancarrow.

"He won't help," replied Bob, disgusted.

Rising, she said, "I will."

Bob and Doreen struggled but eventually got the plane turned. Then they pushed it back as close as they could to where the driver lay, but logs blocked their way and they were still at least a hundred feet from him.

Meanwhile, Willie told the deputy of the plan. The deputy approved and was moving his cruiser to the far end of the straightaway. Willie was also able to enlist the aid of two men who'd been stopped at the roadblock. He followed them to the end of the straightaway so they could park their car, then they joined him in his pickup for the ride back to the accident site. When they arrived, Willie maneuvered his pickup around the airplane and parked. Then he and the two volunteers jumped out and ran to where the driver lay moaning in pain.

Doreen said, "He's getting worse. Let's hurry."

The five of them each grabbed handfuls of the blanket Arnie lay on and, grunting and straining, carried him to the airplane. With a last effort they hoisted him in.

Placing a parachute under Arnie's head, Bob said, "I need someone to come with me and take care of him. Would you do it?" He was asking Doreen.

She had never been in a small plane before. In fact she'd never been in *any* airplane before. And the idea of getting into this one and taking off from a narrow, tree-lined road in the semi-darkness gave her a knot in the pit of her stomach. She stared at Arnie Pelto, then at Bob, then nodded, "Sure. I love to fly," and climbed in.

The takeoff was flawless, in less than a minute they were out of sight. Bob didn't bother climbing to altitude; he didn't want to waste the time. He kept the Six's engine roaring at full throttle and flew a hundred feet above the treetops all the way back to the airport.

Willie watched them depart. As he turned to go to his truck, the man who'd been sitting on the log and not helping walked up and said, "I want your name."

Sensing his tar and nicotine levels were dipping dangerously low, Willie knocked a Marlboro from his pack, lit it, then casually inquired, "Who's asking?"

"I'm Raymond Nancarrow, chairman of the board of the First Northern National Bank. That pilot broke the law and you're a witness. I need your name."

Geez, thought Willie, talk about an alibi.

"Sure. It's Willie . . . Willie Salo."

"Mr. Salo, how can I get ahold of you?"

"Well, I don't have a phone, but I was thinking of doing some banking tomorrow so why don't I get in touch with you?"

"That would be fine. Thank you." Nancarrow paused, then cocked his head in the direction of the Ford. "Say, that's your pickup truck, isn't it?"

"Yup."

"Think you could maneuver your way through these logs?"

"Suppose so. Why?"

"Well, if you could do that, and drive me to my daughter's cottage at the Thunder Bay Club, I'd be very grateful."

Willie saw dollar bills. "How grateful?"

"Would, say, fifty dollars be enough?"

"Mr. Nancarrow, it's not that I don't want to give you a ride, it's just that I'm kind of late for a—"

Nancarrow cut him off with a wave of the hand. "A

hundred dollars. Would a hundred dollars make it worth being a little later?"

Willie had to think about it. It would be at least forty minutes out of his way; his first reaction was not to do it. The hundred bucks was attractive, but wasn't he going to be a millionaire by the end of tomorrow? In the end though it was the idea of spending time with Nancarrow that changed his mind. It seemed so bold and perverse to drive the chairman of the board home knowing he was going to rob his bank the next morning. There was something poetic and dangerous about it. So in the end he said yes.

He and Nancarrow got into the truck and Willie weaved his way through the accident site then motored toward Big Bay. He thought the ride was going to be interesting, but once Nancarrow started talking he wouldn't stop. He went on and on about the pilot and what he had done to him and how he had broken the law and if he had any loans at the bank then he, Raymond Nancarrow, was going to see that they were called due and payable, and that he was going to prosecute him for assault and that he had friends in the Federal Aviation Administration and he'd make sure the pilot lost his license if it was the last thing he ever did, and so on and so forth. After about twenty minutes of this griping Willie had a strong urge to tell him to shut his pie hole, but thought better of it and kept silent. Nancarrow finally ran out of spleen and they drove in silence for awhile. Then an idea popped into Willie's head. Perhaps he could plant some seeds of discord here with Nancarrow that might help encourage Eric do the right thing in the morning.

"Mr. Nancarrow, quite a coincidence running into you like this. I could go a whole year and never see two bankers, and now I see two in one day. That . . . what's his name? . . Derrick Kramer . . ."

"You mean Eric Kramer?"

"Yeah, Eric Kramer. He's the president of the bank isn't he?"

"Yes, Eric is the president."

"Wow, I never thought bankers could party like that. I

was at the Flat Squirrel right before I ran into you folks and he was there whooping it up and slamming down drinks like a pulp cutter on payday."

"Eric Kramer? Are you sure we're talking about the same Eric Kramer? That certainly doesn't sound like him," said Nancarrow, shaking his head.

"Well, I can't swear to it because I don't know him personally, but I sure thought it was him. Tall, blond guy. Well dressed. And the girl pressing new creases in his shirt kept calling him Eric, so I guessed it was him. Hey, I could be wrong, so don't fire him or anything on account of what I said here, okay? But the way he was hammering down those drinks, well, I wouldn't exactly expect him to be to work on time tomorrow . . . if you know what I mean." Willie gave Nancarrow an exaggerated wink to add emphasis to the lie. Nancarrow didn't respond so Willie shut up.

They drove another few miles before turning off on a road that led to the Thunder Bay Club. One gated entry and two miles later they arrived at Nancarrow's daughter's cottage. The "cottage" was about four thousand square feet of varnished, square cut, log home, with French windows, cedar shake roof and a slate patio and walkway. The location was prime, one acre surrounded by an oxbow of one of the slow, sandy rivers that wind their way through the Club. A number of cars were parked in front; the place had the lit up look of a party. Wordlessly, Nancarrow paid him, climbed out of the truck, straightened his bloodstained tie, then carefully lifting his suitcase from the bed of the pickup, mustered as much dignity as he could and strode toward the entrance.

Willie turned the Ford around and headed back toward Marquette and Carmen's. He took 510, making it in just under an hour.

Chapter 36

It took Eric over two hours to walk from Harlow Lake to where the tracks crossed Lakeshore Boulevard in north Marquette, then another forty minutes to slink to his home on Ridge Street. It had become dark during the walk, but the sky was clear and a three-quarter moon provided ample illumination so it didn't matter. He saw no one on the tracks, of course, and took pains to avoid being spotted on his way through Marquette.

Using a key he kept hidden under a planter, he let himself in. Once inside he stripped off his grimy clothes, tossed them into the washer, fixed himself a chicken salad sandwich with romaine on whole wheat, then took a long hot shower. Afterward, he poured a healthy dose of 12 year old Glenlivet scotch into his favorite Waterford glass, dropped in a couple ice cubes and went to the living room to mull over the day's events and decide what to do.

Sitting in the comfort of his Lazy Boy, Eric began what he hoped would be the journey back to normal. Damn, he thought, what a mess. If only my car hadn't broken. It's all Mattson's fault. He's going to pay for this. Picking up the phone, Eric called a tow service and told them where to find the burned Beamer; instructing them to deposit it directly in front of Mattson's showroom window. A sardonic smile crossed his face as he visualized Teddy Mattson's panic when he found it.

The next order of business was Doreen Harmon. She'd witnessed his embarrassment with the car, then left him stranded at the Flat Squirrel. Unbelievable! She couldn't possibly think he'd forgive her. He made a mental note to have her fired first thing in the morning. He'd talk to Janice Richards, the head teller, and find some excuse for "just cause." He didn't want her to be able to collect unemployment against their account. *Not one penny.*

The next item on the agenda was the business about the truck and that fool with the bomb. This was more complicated. How could he handle it? He'd made an ass of himself by having a drink and dancing with that strumpet at the bar. Then her Neanderthal boyfriend had punched him out. Everyone there saw him get dragged outside. Did anyone see him get punched? He wasn't sure, but didn't think so. Maybe that could work in his favor. But what about the truck? His fingerprints were all over it. How long would it take for them to be washed away? Minuets? Years? And if that fruit cake put his wallet inside, he'd definitely be connected to it. The truck was the problem. How could he explain taking the truck without being coerced? He couldn't. And where's the evidence of coercion without the bomb? There isn't any. Therefore, one of two things has to happen: Either the truck needs to remain undiscovered, or he has to tell the police everything. But if he told the whole story, the part about the dumpster would come out. The dumpster episode would stick with him. People would make jokes. It would be hard to live with. It *may* even affect his career. Of course, he could lie. But when the police interview the mutant who dragged him outside, he'll undoubtedly brag about it. Everyone will find out. And when they catch the weasel who put the bomb on him, he'll corroborate the story. There was no way around it. It would all come out. *Christ!* He'd worked so hard to get where he was, and now this, this fluke, this chance occurrence, through no fault of his own, had changed his life. Then he remembered what the controller said:

"Things happen out of the blue. Things that are totally unanticipated. Things that can't be covered by some plan or insurance policy."

Fancy words for a criminal, he thought. But true nonetheless.

He sat still for a while gazing around the room. There was a high ceiling trimmed with ornate crown molding, and buff colored plaster walls, and oak flooring covered by a Persian rug in a subtle brown and black arch design. On Annie's advice he'd furnished the room in chunky Art Deco and decorated the walls with prints of famous oils by Cézanne and Picasso. For pure comfort and indulgence he'd added a brown leather Lazy-Boy recliner. Each and every item being chosen after long deliberation and serious haggling to beat down the price. They were now all familiar things. All important to him and his comfort. Things he did not want to be without. But what if he were to lose them, his home, his job, his standing in the community? What would he do then? Even if he called the police and they caught the loon with the bomb, he was still at some risk from the embarrassing incident at the bar. Damn! It was all so confusing. If only the car hadn't had a problem and he were at Annie's now . . . *ANNIE'S!* "Oh, God! I've got to call her and explain. She'll be hotter than a boiled owl. What can I say? Oh . . . shoot! . . and Ray is there too. Oh, brother, this is going to look bad." His mind flashed again on the controller's words.

"I've never been a bank president, but I'm smart enough to know that even bank presidents have to take crap from somebody. Those chowder-heads you work for, they could get together some day and one could say, 'My little girl Agnes, you know, the ugly one with only one tit, is going out with a nice boy from Harvard, and he sure would like to be a bank president, and Agnes, she sure wants to get married, and . . .' Do you get my drift? This stuff happens all the time."

He had to admit it was a reasonably accurate description of his situation with Annie and her father. And a fairly good description of Annie herself. Even so, he *had* to call her. Eric grabbed the phone and dialed. When she answered he said, "Annie, I'm so—"

"Where have you been?" she interrupted. Then, not waiting, answered her own question. "I guess out having fun with your new friend at the Flat Squirrel bar is more important than seeing us." By *us* he knew she meant her and her father.

Eric sighed inwardly. "Look, Annie, it's not what you think. I—"

"Daddy's plane landed on 550 and there was a big accident and everything's a mess . . . but I'm sure this isn't of any interest to you, because *you* seem to have better things to do than honor your commitments. But I imagine Daddy's going to want to see you at the bank tomorrow, so try not to stay out too late so you can be there on time." With that, she hung up.

"Be there on time? *Be there on time!* I've *never* been late for work in my life. And *she* has the nerve to tell *me* to be there on time? Who does she think she is?" But, of course, he knew. She was the daughter of the chairman of the board. She had his ear. And what ruinous things might she be whispering to him this evening?

"Daddy, when he made love to me he told me I was special, that I was the only woman in his life, and like a fool I believed him, or I wouldn't have done it. He said he loved me. But now he's down at that roadhouse getting drunk with his new girlfriend, after he promised he'd come to my party. Daddy, he knew I was counting on him. He knew you were coming. But he just didn't care."

God! thought Eric, how could things go so wrong.

He refilled his drink, then slumped back down in the chair. It was going to take some tricky explaining and a truckload of extra attention to smooth things over with Annie. He knew he could do it, but certainly didn't relish the task, somewhat belatedly realizing he didn't like her very much. But, of course, he *had* to smooth things over. He couldn't allow her to continue thinking he'd snubbed her. Then, involuntarily, he remembered another thing the controller said.

"Fuck you money. It's so if life has you down or people are giving you a hard time you have enough money to say fuck you and walk away knowing they can't do a damn thing about it because you have plenty of money, enough to do anything you want."

He'd saved quite a bit of his earnings, and with his 401k and the company stock plan he had nearly a $100,000 accumulated. But that certainly wasn't fuck you money. It wasn't even close.

Chapter 37

While waiting for Eric to appear, Carmen had ample time to ponder the wisdom of her renewed alliance with Willie, the merits of his plan, whether it was smart to have let Eric go, and what she would do if they got caught. She knew she could get out now—get out and never be suspected of a thing. Tell Willie thanks but no thanks. Go home, take a hot bath and wile away the hours until Dick returned. She sensed it would be the wise thing to do, but she couldn't bring herself to do it. Because, for all his faults, Willie had something she admired; the courage to be himself. He wasn't afraid to be Willie Salo. He wasn't afraid for people to know exactly who Willie Salo was and what Willie Salo thought. And, if by some miracle this crazy plan of his worked and they got away clean with five million, or even one million, or a half million, that would be enough. They could go somewhere and live easy, and she could stop pretending.

The old Marquette and Huron Mountain railroad tracks intersect Lakeshore Boulevard at the northernmost part of Marquette. Lakeshore then traces the shoreline of Lake Superior south-southeast in a shallow, backward C toward the center of town. Between the water and the road is enough cover, in the form of boulders, shrubs and, in some sections, trees, to keep a man hidden from view. This is the route Carmen watched Eric take as he made his way home.

For Eric, the path he took was neither the easiest nor most direct, but it kept him well hidden from curious eyes. And Carmen wasn't sure whether it meant he was following Willie's plan because he'd bought into it, or because he believed Willie could cause trouble for him with Moose's truck, or because he believed Willie would be watching him, or simply because he looked like a bum and didn't want anyone he knew to see him like that. Whatever the reason, she knew it was far better than him hailing the first car that came along and demanding to be driven to the police station. But she also knew to get to be the president of a bank was not an easy thing. He had to be smart, and aggressive. She was quite certain he wasn't the type who enjoyed taking orders. He'd want to be the one calling the shots.

She watched from a distance as Eric waited till there was no traffic in sight, then crossed Lakeshore Boulevard again and made his way up the hill to his home on Ridge Street. His house turned out to be one of the old and elegant remnants of Marquette's past. The construction was of large, reddish, sandstone blocks of irregular size, which initially gave Carmen the impression of a cold, impregnable fortress, until the interior lights went on and the aura changed to a warm, inviting, secure home that would last forever.

After Eric was inside, Carmen cruised by once then parked around a corner a discreet distance away. If need arose, she could start up and drive off without anyone on Ridge Street noticing. She fully expected to see police cars arriving at Eric's within minutes. But, to her relief, none came. That didn't mean he hadn't called them. But maybe, just maybe, he hadn't. A person without doubts wouldn't hesitate. Or could it be he was simply acting out what he knew Willie wanted to see? Did he call the authorities, explain everything, and request they not come to his home, lights on and sirens blaring, because we might be watching—all to make us believe he was obeying instructions? Would they be following Eric tomorrow when he went to meet Willie? Was the machinery of the law already hard at work dredging up information and sifting through names for possible suspects? Were there unmarked cars patrolling the area now, recording license plates and looking for anyone who might be watching the house? This last thought made her uneasy. How could she explain why she was parked there—on a dark corner in a residential area? She really couldn't. So she decided she'd stay for twenty minutes and not a moment longer. Twenty minutes would be all the anxiety she could handle.

Time dragged by uneventfully. Several cars drove along Ridge Street, but they all appeared to be driven by regular people doing regular things. One young couple walked past the Jeep, but they couldn't have been more than high school age. No police came to Eric's door. And, once home, he didn't go out again—at least not through the front door via Ridge Street. Finally, time up, Carmen started the white Cherokee and headed for home. But on the way, she kept one eye glued to the rearview mirror and took enough turns and side streets to make sure she wasn't tailed.

Cool white light from the moon illuminated her driveway. Willie was already there when she pulled in; sitting on the tailgate of his pickup, smoking a cigarette and drinking a bottle of Sierra Nevada Pale Ale. She sat down next to him.

"I see your taste in beer is improving. Or is it your income that's on the rise these days?"

Willie adjusted a nonexistent tie. "I thought I'd purchase something a little more appropriate to my new station. Drinking Blatz on a yacht would be gauche."

"Ahhh . . . right, your Lordship."

"Things are going to be different from now on, Carmen. You're going to see a different me."

"Not *too* different I hope. I like the you that you are."

"Oh, not that me. I'll always be the *me* me. But there are a couple of things that definitely need changing."

Carmen frowned. "Like what?"

Willie thought for a moment. "Well . . . take my clothes for example. When we're off sailing that yacht around the islands, I certainly won't need these clothes."

"You mean you want some new clothes?"

"No, I mean I won't *need* clothes."

"Hmm . . . that's fine with me. I kind of like watching the pendulum swing. But we *will* have to stop sometime you know, to pick up food and things like that. You can't just run around the marina buck naked. People might whisper."

"Good point. Maybe I'll get one of those real skimpy bathing suits like the fluffy boys wear."

"Ahh . . . I can see you've thought this thing through. Anything else?"

"Yeah. I think I might take the time to learn how to cook."

"Cook! You? Willie, your idea of cooking is opening a can. You need to check the recipe to make toast." Laughing, "I've seen you ask for a second opinion to decide when water is boiling."

"I'm not that bad."

"No? Don't you remember the time you tried to make that venison stew? You ended up throwing the whole thing out behind the cabin. Then that bear came around and ate some. We could hear the poor thing moaning for a week. Willie, I think he *died!* So if you're determined to cook then I think we'd better steal ten million because we'll need at least five for medical bills."

"Oh, okay," he said, mugging a sulk.

Tentatively Carmen inquired, "Anything else? Or dare I ask?"

Willie adopted a thoughtful posture. "Yeah. I thought I might take on an air of eccentricity. That's what rich people do you know."

"Do they?"

"Sure. Take Howard Hughes for example. He used to wash his hands about five hundred times a day and had fingernails a foot long. I'll bet no one ever made the mistake of thinking he punched a time clock."

"How many of those have you had?" teased Carmen, gesturing toward the bottle in his hand.

"I'm just using that as an example," he explained, ignoring the implication. "Maybe I'll grow something else. Maybe nose hair or something like that."

"Bartender, cut this man off."

"I need to develop a style of my own," he continued. "Something to distinguish me; set me apart from the pack."

"Willie, you already *have* a style of your own. You

don't need to change. You're the only Willie Salo in the world. And you're better at being you than anyone else could ever possibly hope to be."

"Come on, Carmen, what's the fun of having a bunch of money if you can't be eccentric?"

"Oh all right," she said. "But not the nose hair. Something a little more subtle."

"Ear hair."

"Fine, ear hair. But only natural growth, no steroids. Deal?"

"Deal."

They went back and forth like that for a while before Willie turned serious and asked, "How'd it go in town?"

"He did exactly what you told him. Going home he went out of his way not to be seen. And when he got there he stayed there. I hung around for twenty minutes, and no cops showed up. Doesn't mean he didn't call them, but at least it doesn't mean he did."

Willie told her about the events which took place on his way to Big Bay.

"Geez, you must have been scared to death."

"Nah. Cool as a cucumber."

"And Doreen is okay?" Then, catty. "Did you comfort her in her time of need?"

"Yes, she's fine. And *no*, Carmen, I didn't comfort her in her time of need. Heck, she was making goo-goo eyes at the pilot all the time I was there. I'll bet if he hadn't asked her to fly back with him she would have roped herself to the wing."

Then Willie told her about the business with Nancarrow.

"Seems like a smart move would be to make sure our friend, Eric, is late for work tomorrow," said Carmen. "He's bound to get a good spanking when he gets there, and that should make him just that much more anxious to behave for us."

Willie rubbed his chin. "Hmm . . . does seem to be sort of

a problem that Nancarrow will be there tomorrow. Means Eric won't really be in charge, Nancarrow will."

"That's right. Look, I want to get this thing over with as badly as you do, but it might be better to wait till Monday morning. That is, assuming Nancarrow won't be there Monday too. And, a little extra time could help in other ways. Think of it, Willie, the more time that goes by without Eric talking to the police, if he hasn't already, the harder it will be for him to explain why he waited. And maybe we could manufacture a few more crimes for him to commit so he'll feel he's in deeper. If only there were some way to make Nancarrow really mad at him. I think that would cause Eric to start seeing things in a whole new light."

"You're making a lot of sense, hon." He paused for a sip of beer. "I think it would be helpful to have more information about Eric. If we knew more about him it would be easier to push the right buttons to get him to do what we want."

"Hmm . . . yes. As much as I hate to say it, maybe you should call up your pal, Doreen. She works at the bank, doesn't she?"

"Yes, she does. Never talks about it much though. Just says it's boring."

"You never know," said Carmen. Then, conspiratorially, "I want to tell you a secret, Willie." She moved closer. "Now if I tell, you won't go blabbing it all over will you?"

Willie's eyebrows went up a half inch. "A secret? Like what?"

"If I tell you, you have to promise not to tell."

"I promise," he replied, giving the Boy Scout sign.

Carmen leaned closer and whispered, "Sometimes when women get together they talk."

"Huh! You mean there are times when they don't talk?"

"And sometimes when they talk, it's about men."

"Stop the presses."

"And sometimes even about the boss," finished Carmen.

It took Willie a moment to fully digest this bit of wisdom. Then he tossed down what remained of his beer and said, "Let's find out."

When they entered the house and Carmen turned the lights on, Willie was immediately impressed. The living room was easily as large his entire cabin. A cathedral ceiling paneled in beveled cedar led to textured walls painted a warm off-white, on which hung a variety of oil paintings depicting western landscapes and cowboys at work. The furniture continued the western theme with an expensive-looking leather-covered couch and matching easy chairs all resting on a Navajo rug. At one end of the room was a large stone fireplace with stonework extending through the ceiling. The other end the room was thrust outward in the middle forming two sides of a triangle made of tall rectangular windows trimmed with cedar to match the ceiling. Willie guessed in the daytime the windows provided a spectacular view of the Nash River Basin and the hills beyond. He estimated the windows alone were probably worth more than his cabin, and the thought depressed him. Turning away from them, he following Carmen into a bright modern kitchen. In the middle was a butcher block island with several bar stools. Willie pulled one out and tentatively sat down. In his entire life he'd never been in a home as nice as this one; it made him feel disoriented and out of place.

Then his thoughts went to Carmen and about her willingness to give it up, the house and everything else, for him. He wondered if he was making a terrible mistake by involving her in his scheme and placing her at such risk. Things could go wrong. She could lose the easy life she had, and much, much more. He did not want that to happen.

"Nice digs, Carmen. You sure you want to give this up?"

She replied without hesitation. "I'm sure."

Carmen handed him a phone and Willie dialed the number. Doreen answered on the third ring.

"Hey, Doreen. Just wanted to call and see if you're all right."

"That's nice of you, Willie. Thanks for calling." She said it as though "and good bye" were tacked on the end.

"Yeah, I was kind of in a state of shock out there and I,

ah . . . well . . . say, how's that truck driver doing? Did he make it okay?"

"We're not sure yet. The ambulance people didn't say much when they took him, but the way they were looking at him and hurrying, well . . . I just don't know. Robert and I are going over to the hospital tomorrow to see if he's okay."

"Robert? Who's Robert? . . Oh . . . the midget pilot."

"No, Willie, the *brave* pilot. If it weren't for him I'd hate to think of what might have happened."

Willie wanted to say something less complementary, but forced himself to say, "Yeah, he seemed like a pretty good guy."

"And?"

"What and?"

"I know you better than that."

"No, really. He took charge out there and got everybody moving. Heck, if it weren't for him nobody woulda done a thing."

"That's right. He probably saved my life. And Arnie's too."

Willie heard somebody say something in the background, and Doreen responded, "You *did*, Robert. If it weren't for you we could have been killed!"

"Am I interrupting something?"

"Well . . . it was getting late and neither of us had eaten, so I invited Robert over for dinner."

"What's for dessert?"

"Geez . . . You're hopeless."

"Come on . . . I was kidding. Actually I'm glad he's there."

"You are?"

"Yeah. You know that other guy, the one whose butt was glued to the log all the time we were saving the truck driver?"

"We?"

"Hey, I helped too!"

"Okay, okay, that's right. Yes, I remember him."

"Do you know who that was?"

"No. Should I?"

"Well I would think so. He runs the bank you work at."

"What are you talking about? Mr. Kramer is the president of the bank."

"Kramer may be the president, Doreen, but that guy, Nancarrow, is the chairman of the board. That makes him Kramer's boss."

"Are you sure?"

"As sure as it gets. That's all he talked about on the way to the Thunder Bay Club."

"You drove him up to the Thunder Bay Club?"

"Yeah. We got to talking and he said, 'Would you drive me up to the Thunder Bay Club?' I said, 'Oh sure, glad to.' And we had a nice chat on the way up. But mostly he wanted to talk about Kramer. He went on about how he might not be doing such a good job and how they might have to replace him and that sort of stuff."

"He told you that? Why? Why would he tell you?"

"Oh, maybe he just wanted to bounce it off of someone who didn't have an axe to grind. You know, no vested interest in the bank."

"He must have seen your balance. Or maybe he was in shock."

"What do you think, Doreen? What's the word you hear? Is Kramer doing a good job? Or is he screwing up all the time like Raymond said?"

"You're on a first name basis with him?"

"Sure. He wanted me to come in and have a drink and meet the folks at his daughter's birthday party. I kind of wanted to, but I was a little tired so I told him maybe next time."

"Oh, gosh! So that's why he was all worried about getting up to the Thunder Bay Club."

"Huh?"

"Mr. Kramer. I was driving up 550 and saw him on the side of the road. He'd had some car trouble. I guess something started burning because the car was smoking like crazy. So I gave him a ride to the Flat Squirrel and . . . and then left him there."

"Shrewd career move, Doreen."

"Geez. With everything that's happened tonight I'd almost forgotten. Oh boy . . . he's going to be sooo mad."

"You never know. Maybe he'll get lucky at the Squirrel and thank you the next time he sees you."

"I don't think so. When I picked him up he was real upset. He has this beautiful, new, gray BMW and it broke down. He said he had an important party he had to go to at the Thunder Bay Club. *That* must have been the party—a birthday party for the chairman of the board's daughter. No wonder he was so worked up. And while we were driving up there he said he needed to make a phone call. He'd been such a jerk that I thought I'd have a little fun at his expense, so I brought him to the Flat Squirrel. Figured he'd feel like a fish out of water there. I waited at the bar for him for a half hour and then saw him out on the dance floor with some blond, dancing away like he didn't have a care in the world. So I left."

"Is he the vindictive type?"

"I'll say. Nobody crosses Mr. Kramer."

"He must be a hard guy to work for."

"Well, I really don't see him that much. I mean, he struts around at the bank to make sure everything's going okay, but he usually only talks to the people right beneath him, you know, like the head teller. Then she tells us what he wants, or what he's all upset about. He's real particular about everything. But he hardly ever talks to us personally."

"So what's his thing? You know, what's his personal life like."

"I don't know anything about his personal life, but it's probably pretty boring. The guy's so full of himself, who could stand to be around him? Probably spends most his free time in front of a mirror."

"Anything else?"

"Other than being a big jerk, I don't think so. Why?"

"Oh. Just curious."

"Well, Willie, this has been fun, but I really have to go. Thanks for calling."

"Yeah, don't mention it. And, ah, just an FYI. I wouldn't start picking out the colors for the nursery just yet because your new boyfriend is about to go out of business."

"What? What are you talking about?"

"Ol' Nancarrow was pissed. *Really* pissed. Guess it had something to do with landing the plane on the road. He told me he was going to call in all of Robert the brave pilot's loans and make sure he loses his license, and said he's gonna sic his attorneys on him and sue his ass into bankruptcy. . . I'm talking *major* pissed off."

"You're making that up."

"I'm not. I'm telling you because you and I are friends, and you seem to have a thing for him. Come tomorrow morning the brown stuff's going to hit the spinning blade and he's going to be Robert the unemployed pilot."

"You're jealous."

"Okay, Doreen, think what you like. But tomorrow when you find out what I said is true, I hope you'll be big enough to say you're sorry."

Carmen heard his side of the conversation, and when he was done Willie filled in the blanks. They ate roast beef sandwiches, drank Sierra Nevada and mulled it over. In the end they came up with three things from the conversation: First, Kramer is real particular about everything. Second, he drives a new BMW that had a problem. And third, this evening he was on his way to Nancarrow's daughter's birthday party. It wasn't much in the way of information, but it was something.

Willie went out to his truck and brought back his road stash—which he always kept hidden in the glove box, on top of his insurance and registration. They got a little high and kicked around some ideas, but nothing came of it except a nagging feeling that Eric was going to call the police in the morning—if he hadn't already.

After an hour or so they ran out of talk and sex seemed the only alternative. The lovemaking turned out to be somewhat listless—almost a mistake. In the past, sex had been a fun game, an adventure in which verbal thrusting and parrying ultimately led to the more physical kind. They'd spent long afternoons, evenings and sometimes entire days being adult children playing with the most fun toys possible, each other. But not this night. For although Carmen did not love Dick Hodges, she did have a certain respect for him, and couldn't get past the feeling she was insulting him by making love to Willie in his very bed. Anywhere else would have been fine, but not there. For his part, Willie kept expecting to hear a door open and someone call out, "Honey, I'm home!" Apart from the distinct possibility of violence, it would, at the very least, have been extremely difficult to explain. Willie tried to think of what a person might say under such circumstances. *"Gee, Mr. Hodges, I was just driving by and I heard a woman screaming and I rushed in and I saw her lying there on the bed in agony and I thought maybe it might be demonic possession, so I took off all my clothes and . . ."* No, there wasn't much you could say. And, for both of them, at the wrong moments their thoughts would drift to the day's activities and the uncertain future which lay ahead.

When it was over they lay silent for a long time till Willie finally spoke. "Carmen, I gotta go out. It's not good enough like this. I know it and you know it. I was stupid to let him go. Kramer will wake up in his own bed in his own house tomorrow, think it over and decide he's better off taking his chances with the cops than with us. Being responsible is his thing. He's been conditioned to obey the rules. When he wakes up he'll know what he has to do. He'll call the cops and then this thing will never happen. I can't let him do that."

"What are you going to do?" asked Carmen, worried.

"I've got some ideas, but I better keep them to myself. Carmen, one thing I realized today that I've never fully understood before is how much I care for you. I'm not sure I've ever loved anyone, and I'm not sure exactly how to act, but one thing I do know is that if the worst happens, if this thing goes wrong, bad wrong, I don't want you involved. And if it goes right I want you involved all the way. So I'm gonna leave now and take care of some details, tie up some loose ends, and try to ratchet up the pressure to keep our banker buddy off balance till it's time for the big payday. And, for your own protection, and because it might be the only noble thing I ever do in my life, I don't want you to know anything about it."

He dressed and left. There were things to be done and only about eight hours to do them. He'd have to act fast if he wanted to get any sleep at all. That is, if he *could* sleep.

Willie lit up a fresh joint and drove to town, taking the main artery, Washington Street, all the way in to where it met Front Street near the lake. There, on the northwest corner of the intersection, was the polished marble facade of the First Northern National Bank. Solid and stately. Slowing, he appraised the structure, then turned south on Front. A couple blocks later he hung right on Spring Street toward where the auto dealerships were clustered. He drove till he spotted Mattson's lot, went another block and parked in an area with no street light. Then he walked back to Mattson's. One look was all he needed to find what he was searching for: A slate-gray BMW was parked directly in front of the showroom.

The smell of burned undercoating told him he had the right vehicle. Using Eric's keys, he unlocked the car. Then, pulling on a pair of work gloves he'd brought from his truck, he opened the door, slid in, and quietly pulled the door shut. Checking first to make sure all the windows were rolled up tight, he fired up his partially used joint and smoked it till there was only a third or so left, adding a heavy layer of pot odor over the rank burned smell inside. He made sure to knock about half of the ashes in the ashtray and the other half on the floor nearby. Then he set the roach neatly in the tray, as if ready for further use.

Before leaving Carmen's, Willie'd gone to the kitchen and pulled a fresh baggie from a pack he found in a drawer. On the way into town he'd stopped in a safe spot, wiped the baggie clean of fingerprints, transferred about an eighth ounce of his road weed into the new container, wrapped a rubber band around it and shoved it in his pocket. He now he pulled it out, gave it an air kiss goodbye and gently placed it on the middle of the passenger seat. He felt some remorse at having to leave the weed, but rationalized that it was for a greater good.

The car was thick with pungent smoke, and when Willie exited he did so quickly to trap most of it inside. He walked around the vehicle to make sure both doors were locked, stopped momentarily to admire his work, mentally patted himself on the back, then turned away and strolled casually back to his green Ford.

Happier now that he'd done something, he drove through town to Wright Street and turned north on 550 headed toward the Squirrel. Arriving, he surveyed the parking lot. After finding out what he needed to know, he left the lot and turned south. About three miles later he pulled off on a curvy dirt trail that led to nowhere and parked. Getting out, he unhooked a two-gallon gas can that was bungeed to the bed of the pickup. After checking the highway to make sure no one was coming, he ran up 550 to a driveway leading to a small house. The house belonged to Moose McCullough.

Willie checked the door and found, as expected, it was unlocked. Gathering his courage, he went in, turned on the lights, found the bedroom, then rummaged around until he discovered what he was looking for . . . a handgun. He didn't own a gun and he didn't particularly like them, but he felt he needed to have one now—just in case. Tucking the gun in his trousers, he went to the kitchen and searched until he found Moose's stock of liquor and appropriated a nearly full bottle of Jack Daniels whisky. Then he turned off the lights and went back outside to where he'd left the can of gasoline. After unscrewing the cap, he set about splashing gasoline all over the front of the house, and with the last few ounces made a trail of fuel eight feet up the walk. Pulling Eric's wallet from his pocket, he tossed it a few feet further up the walk. Then he flicked his lighter and with a swoosh the entire front of Moose McCullough's house was engulfed in flames.

Willie ran full speed to his pickup, cranked it up and barreled south to a small convenience store located several miles beyond Wetmore's Landing in the direction of Marquette. The store was closed, but there was a pay phone outside. He used it to call the fire department and anonymously report what appeared to be a serious house fire several miles south of the Flat Squirrel.

Willie drove the rest of the way to Marquette sipping Jack Daniels as he went. It was 1:30 in the morning and he was getting tired, but there was more yet to do. He cruised past Eric's darkened house, went a half block more, then parked the truck and doubled back on foot. When he got to the house he crept up the front steps, removed Eric's keys from his pocket and gently hung them from the doorknob on a length thread he'd pulled from the old gray towel in his truck He wanted to make sure Eric would find his keys in the morning on his way out. Task done, he returned again to his truck.

"Just a couple more things," he said to himself. "A couple more details."

Driving to a secluded pay phone west of town, he checked the directory. Finding the number he wanted, he dialed.

Eight rings later he heard a sleepy "Hello?"

In his best imitation of a drunken Eric Kramer he slurred, "Annnee, Annnneee, Annneeee, ish thaaat youu?"

"Who is this?"

"Annneeee, ish meee, Herricck."

"Good God! You're *drunk*. Why don't you go home and try to sleep it off. You can call me in the morning. But make sure you're sober first. Good night."

That was it. He'd done everything he could do alone that might be useful on Saturday morning. But there was one last thing, something he would need Carmen's help with, so he drove to Carmen's again and found her up watching a late movie.

"Where'd you go?" she asked.

"I'd rather not say," he replied. Then added, "It's for your own protection."

"Okay. But I'm with you all the way, Willie, for better or worse. I want you to know that."

"I know you are, hon, and I need your help with one last detail."

"Sure, what?"

"Remember earlier when I was talking to Doreen, she said Kramer was dancing with a blond."

"Yeah?"

"And later on we see Moose toss him in the dumpster."

"Okay?"

"It doesn't take a genius to figure out who that blond was."

Driving through dark streets to a pay phone, Willie explained what he wanted her to say. Carmen rehearsed her lines a couple of times and was ready when they got there. Willie dialed, and when Annie Nancarrow answered, Carmen said, "Hello, is Eric there?"

"Eric? Who are you calling?"

"Eric Kramer, that's who. I need to talk to him. It's important. Is he there? If he is let me talk to him. I'm afraid of what he'll do?"

"Do? What do you mean?"

"He got in a fight and got beat up. Now I think he's going to do something crazy."

"How did you get this number?"

"I pushed redial. I thought you might be a friend of his and could help me out. I've never seen anyone so angry. Please, if he's there let me talk to him."

"Who are you?"

"My name's Sheila. After the fight we came over here to my place and had a couple of drinks, but then he started talking about the fight and got real mad and asked if he could borrow my car and left. Then I got to thinking maybe it wasn't such a good idea, me letting him have it, on account of him being so drunk and angry and all. I remembered he called someone while he was here. I guess it was you. So that's why I'm calling. I'm worried sick about what he might do."

"Well, ah, Sheila, if I were you I wouldn't worry one bit about Eric Kramer. I can assure you I won't. And please don't call here again." With that, Annie Nancarrow hung up.

Willie drove Carmen back to her house. She wanted him to stay, but he declined saying he didn't feel right sleeping in Dick's house and in Dick's bed and he'd better go back to his cabin and get some rest because tomorrow was going to be a big day. He gave Carmen instructions regarding what he wanted her to do in the morning, kissed her and left.

Willie made it back to his cabin a little after three in the morning. It felt good to be home, and he realized, one way or the other, this might be the last night he would ever spend there. The thought was strangely depressing. The cabin, which had for so long seemed like a prison and symbol of his failure, suddenly seemed a haven; a place where he was truly king and answered to no man. Sitting in one of the mismatched chairs at his old kitchen table he thought about this and bits and pieces of other things great and small, but was so tired that he only stayed up for one beer, a couple shots of Jack and half of a joint before finally capping the bottle and falling asleep fully dressed on the couch.

Chapter 38

As he awoke, Eric's first thought was, I can't be late for work. Going through his morning cleaning and feeding ritual he mulled over the events of the past day. The effects of the drinks at the Squirrel, being punched in the face, wearing a bomb, walking nearly ten miles and spending hours in soggy stinking clothes had, for the most part, passed. Being safely in his own dwelling, taking a hot shower, eating good food, sleeping in his own soft bed and dressing in an expensive, conservatively-styled suit had brought him back to reality; and reality was that he was the president of the First Northern National Bank. He had standing and credibility in the community, and when he went to the police he would be believed. He'd done nothing wrong, nothing illegal. He had, perhaps, shown some bad judgment there at the bar, but other than that his conduct was beyond reproach. Smiling inwardly, he was amused he'd even for a moment considered the possibility of entering into a criminal conspiracy with that fool with the bomb. *Ridiculous!* He had everything he'd ever wanted . . . everything except a great deal of money. And over time that too would come.

Eric had planed on calling the police from home before work, but a tap on the snooze button had cost him the opportunity. Since it was important to tell them the whole story in great detail, and not be rushed, he decided to call them from his office instead. As important as it was to call the police, it wasn't even a close second to arriving at the bank on time. He assumed Nancarrow would be by for a visit, perhaps early, and he couldn't run the risk of arriving late. Nancarrow had a volatile temper. Eric could only imagine what Annie might have said to him. No sense taking any chances, bank first, police second. Then, as he opened his front door to leave, he heard a jingling and looked down to see his keys swinging on a thread from the doorknob. "What the . . ?" That fool has been here, thought Eric. He must think he's real clever. I'll show him clever. Eric pocketed the keys and hurried off to the bank.

Chapter 39

T here was a smile on her face when she awoke, and she thought she might be in love. He was so nice. He was charming and funny and down to earth. And so handsome and intelligent and brave. And best of all, he seemed to like her too. She'd fixed dinner. They'd talked for hours. It all felt so natural. So right. As he was leaving, when they were at the door, he asked her if he could kiss her. Of course she said yes. She could still feel the electricity. Then, thinking about the accident, she quipped, "If I had known that's what it would take to find a good man I would have crashed my car a lot sooner."

Even the thought of going to the bank and what might await her there couldn't spoil her mood. Three hours, she thought. Three short hours and I'll be off work and driving to Curly Field. Bob had asked her if she'd like to meet him there. He was hauling parachute jumpers and invited her to come along for the ride. Afterward he'd take her on a scenic tour of the area and then out to dinner. It sounded wonderful. He was wonderful. And there was nothing Eric Kramer could do to her today—yell at her, fire her, tie her to an ATM machine and beat her with a chain—nothing at all that would spoil her mood. As she finished getting ready she glanced in the mirror, smiled and said, "I think Doreen's in love." She felt fabulous. It was another beautiful day, and she was going to enjoy it to the fullest.

Arriving at quarter to nine, Doreen spent some time chatting outside with the other employees. The minutes went by quickly. She tensed as the guard opened the door to let them in. Here it comes, she thought. But nothing came. Mr. Kramer was there right at nine sharp and acting perfectly normal; that is, he didn't say a word to anybody, went straight to his office, and stayed there. As the minutes went by and nothing happened, she began to relax. Maybe Willie was right, she thought. Maybe he *did* have a good time at the Squirrel last night.

Chapter 40

A woodpecker was furiously hammering on an old, resonant pine tree. Pileated, guessed Willie. Had to be one of those big suckers to make so much racket. Then, who he was, where he was, and the events of the previous day, jolted him awake like a pail of ice water. The cabin was bathed in light. "Mother of God! What time is it?" Checking his watch, "Eight-thirty! I gotta get going."

Damn, damn, damn! he thought. Now I've really screwed up. I shoulda got up early to get Kramer out of his routine . . . delay him so he'd be late for work. But now that's down the crapper. He grabbed a half-empty bag of potato chips and a warm Coke and bolted for the pickup. Twenty-five minutes later he was at a pay phone in Marquette.

"Did you do it, Carmen?"

"Just what you told me," came the reply.

"What happened?"

"I drove into town and used a pay phone to call the paper like you said. Then I went over by Mattson's and waited. Sure enough, in about fifteen minutes a reporter and photographer showed up. I was pretty far away so I couldn't hear what they were saying, but they walked around the car and took a bunch of pictures. I made the call at seven-thirty sharp and the newspaper people were already there checking out the car for about ten minutes before the first employee came to unlock the place. They talked with him for awhile and talked to the other employees as they arrived. After that the cops came. Then Mattson showed up. He had a guy work on the car door till it opened. After that they took turns looking inside, and the photographer took a lot of pictures. All in all, the people from the paper must have hung around about forty-five minutes before they finally took off. And, for what it's worth, they were smiling when they left. Did I do good, Willie?"

"Sure did, babe. Guess we'll have to wait and see, but something tells me today is going to be a big news day in Marquette."

Willie drove to a different pay phone, then called the bank. "Hello, could I speak to Mr. Kramer."

"Who should I say is calling?"

"Tell him it's . . . Mr. Harlow."

Willie was shunted to ignore for a minute or so before hearing Eric's voice. "Hello, this is Eric Kramer."

"It's show time, Eric. Ready to have some fun?"

"Listen you nitwit, I'm not putting on any bomb or robbing any bank. And the only reason you're not in jail right now is I simply haven't had time to call the police."

"So call them, mister truck thief. Go ahead."

"I *will* go ahead. I'll call them right now after you get off the phone. They'll find out who you are, and then you'll spend the rest of your prime years wondering if it's safe to bend over and pick up the soap."

Willie tossed him a curve ball. "How's your day going?"

"What?"

"I said, how's your day going? What I mean is, you were a naughty boy last night, Eric, and now you're gonna have some '*splainin*' to do."

"What are you talking about? I don't have any '*splainin*' to do. You'll be the one doing the '*splainin*'. Maybe you can entertain the detectives in the interrogation room with your nifty Latin accent."

"Tisk, tisk. You certainly are testy today. Well, if you're not ready then you're not ready. I'm not the pushy kind of bomber who wants to force people into doing what they don't want to do. So I'll just go home and read a magazine or something. See you around." And with that, Willie hung up.

Chapter 41

Nancarrow arrived at the bank at 9:15 with a sore nose and a full head of steam. He went straight to Eric's office, entering without knocking. Eric was just hanging up the phone.

"Have a good time last night, Kramer?" growled Nancarrow.

"What? What do you mean?" asked Eric, trying hard not to stare at the swollen, discolored nose.

"You know exactly what I mean. Annie was expecting you at her birthday party. But instead you spent the night whooping it up at the Flat Squirrel—the *Flat Squirrel* of all places. And then had the *nerve* to call her and make excuses."

"Ray, my car broke down. I was able to get a ride to the Flat Squirrel but was stranded there. I called Annie to tell her I'd be late. Then, one thing led to another and I . . . I couldn't make it. I called later to apologize, but she didn't want to listen. I'm sorry. I truly am."

"Maybe you could have found a way if you hadn't been so drunk."

"Drunk? I wasn't drunk."

"That's not what your friend Susie or Sally or whatever her name was said."

"Sheila?" As soon as the name left his lips he regretted saying it.

"Yes, Sheila, that's it. She said you were drunk and looking for a fight. *And* that you'd been mighty nice to her."

"What? . . Ray, I hardly know her. I just met—"

"Look, Kramer, I don't really give a damn where you park your johnson. But when my daughter's feelings are involved it's a different matter. And I sure as hell don't like it when you start giving out Annie's phone number to the floozies you pick up. How do you think she felt when this Sheila called her at two o'clock in the morning worried about her drunken boyfriend, Eric, who got into a fight and was out looking for revenge?"

"Huh? I didn't . . ." stammered Eric.

"This bank has an image to maintain," fumed Nancarrow. "And barroom brawling isn't part of it. *Jesus*, Kramer, I thought you had more sense than that. And regarding Annie, that's my daughter we're talking about, *and you'd damned well better be nice to her!*"

Eric was stunned. He saw his career in the most tenuous of terms. He knew his best hope hinged on a humiliating extravaganza of sucking up to both Ray and Annie. It would take months, maybe years, to undo the damage and put this behind him. He knew with grave certainty that Ray had enough clout on the board to have him dismissed. All Ray would have to say is that he'd been out drinking and fighting. That would be more than enough. He'd have his walking papers and be gone.

Nancarrow switched gears. "Kramer, I want you to pull all the loans we have with Hart Aviation and that miserable excuse of a pilot, Robert Hart. I want you to call in those loans today."

"Sure, but why?"

"Hart's about to lose his license and go out of business. I want to get back as much on the dollar as we can before anyone else gets into the act. Understand?"

"Of course, Ray. I'll do it right now."

"I'll be in the conference room making some calls. Soon as you get that information bring me a summary. And, Kramer, have your secretary call United and cancel my Monday flight back to Chicago. Looks as though things have gotten fouled up around here and need some straightening out. I have a ten o'clock golf game today, but I'll be here at nine sharp starting Monday."

Eric's heart sank.

"Did you hear me, Kramer?"

"Of course, sir. I'm on it." He said this in his most efficient and business-like voice.

Nancarrow eyed him with disgust, shook his head, then left the office.

Eric immediately called Andrew Malette. Malette was vice president and next in the chain of command at the bank. He ordered Malette to pull up all the loans for Bob Hart and Hart Aviation and bring a summary to Nancarrow at once.

"We're a little short handed this morning, Eric. Can't this wait till Monday?"

"If I wanted it *Monday* I'd have asked for it *Monday*," barked Eric. "Right away," responded Malette.

Then Eric sat still and tried to think. "Reason this thing through," he said softly to himself. "I can find a solution. What I need is an excuse, something to get me off the hook with Nancarrow. He wants me to cancel his flight. He's not going back to Chicago. He's going to stick around and second-guess me on every last decision for God knows how long."

A few minutes later, at 9:30, Eric's secretary buzzed him. "Mr. Kramer, there's a Ms. Fields here to see you. She's a newspaper reporter from the Journal. Should I send her in? She says it's important."

"I'm very busy this morning, Linda. What's this in regard to?"

"She says it's a private matter."

Eric did a long, slow exhale. "Show her in. But tell her it'll have to be brief."

Two beats later his door opened and the reporter walked in. Laura Fields was an attractive woman in her mid twenties with intelligent eyes and dark hair that hung below her shoulders. Her smile was friendly and seemed to say relax and tell me everything, it's going to come out anyway and the public might as well have your side of the story too, don't you think?

"Hi, Miss Fields. Have a seat," said Eric, gesturing to a sturdy Hepplewhite chair in front of his desk.

"Thanks."

When she was seated, he asked, "What can I do for you today?"

"Mr. Kramer, let me get right to the point. Do you own a gray BMW?"

"Yes. Yes I do."

"Did you have some car trouble yesterday and have it towed to Mattson's dealership?"

"That's correct. Why?"

"Did you lock your car before it was towed?"

"Of course. It ah . . . well, it caught on fire as I was driving north on County Road 550 late yesterday afternoon, and I had to leave it on the side of the road. I couldn't leave it there unlocked. That wouldn't be prudent."

"Of course not," agreed the reporter. "So it was locked?"

"I just told you it was. What are you getting at? What's the problem?"

"Just a couple more questions if I may, Mr. Kramer. Were the windows rolled up?"

"It wouldn't make much sense to lock the doors if the windows were rolled down."

"I guess not, Mr. Kramer. So the windows were up?"

"Yes, the windows were up. Now what's the point?"

"Does anyone else have a set of keys to your car?"

"No, only me."

"Do you have the keys to your car, Mr. Kramer?"

"Of course, they're right here." He tapped his suit coat pocket.

"Mr. Kramer, this morning when the employees arrived at Mattson's they found a bag of marijuana in your car. Do you have any idea of how it could have gotten in there?"

Kramer's mouth fell open. "A bag of marijuana? You must be joking? Not in *my* car. There must be a mistake."

"I don't think so, Mr. Kramer. Is your license plate ah . . ." she pulled a pad out of her purse and flipped to an ear-marked page, "BDH933?"

"Yes, that's right. But there couldn't be any marijuana in my car."

"I'm afraid there is, sir. Ah, well actually, was. I believe it's at the police station now. But the police found it in your car. And they found a partially smoked marijuana cigarette. And, along with the burned odor from the fire, the car smelled of marijuana smoke too. So, I guess the last question I have is, since the doors were locked and the windows rolled up and you're the only one with the keys, if the pot wasn't there when you locked the car, then how did it get in there?"

Eric chewed on his lip for several seconds, then he shook his head. "Well, that's a mystery, Miss Fields. Maybe the tow truck driver put it in there, or maybe someone at Mattson's did, or someone else, but I can assure you it wasn't in there when I left the car on 550. I don't smoke marijuana, and I wouldn't knowingly allow anyone who had the stuff to get in my car. Perhaps it was put there yesterday when the car was being worked on at Mattson's?"

"The bag was sitting on the passenger's seat. In full view. Do you think that's something you'd overlook?"

"On the passenger's seat?"

"Right in the middle of it. In full view."

"Geez, I can't explain it. But I'm telling you it isn't mine."

"I asked the mechanics who worked on your car yesterday if they saw anything in there. They said no. I also asked if they'd smelled anything in there like marijuana smoke. They claimed they hadn't. But today, when a locksmith opened the car, the bag was there and a half-smoked joint was in the ash tray and the car reeked of pot. Sure seems like the last person driving that car was smoking pot—wouldn't you say?"

"I can see the implication, Miss Fields. But again, I can assure you it wasn't there when I left the car. Someone must have planted it there after I left it on 550."

"Why would they do that?"

Eric was certain he knew, and he was furious beyond words, but he couldn't tell the reporter and didn't want her to see his anger. Struggling to keep his composure, in his most pleasant voice said, "I can see how this looks. But, after the police investigate, I'm sure they'll find it wasn't mine. And, hopefully, they'll find out who put it there and arrest him. But, in the meantime, if this thing gets in the paper it isn't going to look very good for me. I'm sure you're aware of that. I'm the president of a bank, and even though the stuff isn't mine, and I'm certain the guilty party will be found, the mere suggestion of drug use will create an enormous amount of trouble for both the bank and myself—the kind of trouble that no retraction at a later date could ever repair. With that in mind, do you think there's any way we could keep this out of the paper?"

Fields shook her head. "Mr. Kramer, there's absolutely no way folks aren't going to find out about this. People love to gossip, and when they do they usually emphasize the negative. The people who know you and like you won't re-peat the story, but the people who don't know you or simply don't like you will frame it in the worst possible light. Then they'll run out and tell everyone they see. You're better off, much better off, if the story comes out in the paper. That way the public can hear your side of it first."

He didn't know what to do. He was damned if he did and damned if he didn't. She was right of course, the story would come out either way. He could see it now—COPS BUST DOPE-SMOKING BANKER. True or not, the story would stick like glue.

"You're right of course. But if you could only hold off on the story until Monday it would give the police some time to figure this thing out, and perhaps save me a great deal of trouble and embarrassment. Would you do that for me, Miss Fields?"

Fields thought about it, then raised her hands in a ges-ture of surrender. "Okay. I can sympathize with your situa-tion, Mr. Kramer. I want to give you the benefit of the doubt. I'll check with my editor. If he agrees, we'll wait until Mon-day to print it. And, if you'd like, I'll stop by Monday morn-ing to see if you have anything additional to say. You might think of something important to add to what you've already told me. Would that be all right?"

"That's very kind of you, Miss Fields. I certainly hope

this is all cleared up by Monday. And I'd be very happy to give you a full statement then."

Rising to leave, Fields said, "It's not that big a deal you know. Lots of people smoke pot."

"I'm sure they do, Miss Fields. I'm just not one of them."

The reporter left, and Eric sat in his oak paneled office kneading his face as visions of homicide danced like black-cloaked wraths through his mind. The controller was applying pressure; trying to make sure he'd want some money for himself if things went wrong at the bank. And things were definitely going to go wrong in a very big way if he couldn't prove the dope wasn't his. If he had only called the police last night he wouldn't be in this jam. But he hadn't, and now it was too late. Who was going to believe him about the bomb now? They'd think he'd manufactured the story to cover up for the drugs. "I'll kill him," cursed Eric. "He's ruining my life. I'll kill him if I find him." The intercom interrupted his brutal reverie.

"Mr. Kramer, it's Mr. Harlow on the phone again."

Balling his fists, Eric hissed, "Put... him... through."

"Hey, dude. What's happening?"

The cheerfulness of Willie's inquiry was astonishingly irritating. Eric pressed the phone to his ear and with every fiber of his being willed the party on the other end of the line to die.

"Say, Eric, I sense you're a bit peeved?"

"Do... you... know... what... you... have... done?"

"Who? Me? I haven't done anything. I've been hanging around the house reading the latest issue of Popular Explosives."

"Drugs, you imbecile. *You* put *drugs* in my car."

"Not me, pal. Must have been one of your kinky friends." Willie paused a beat. "You should drop them and start hanging around with a better class of people . . . like me."

"Ohhh . . . I see . . . banker and bottom dweller. Yes . . . I'm sure we'd have a lot in common."

"You don't get it, do you? Take a good look at the people you've surrounded yourself with. They don't give a rat's patooti about you."

"As if you do."

"At least I don't dump my friends for being themselves. Blowing off a little steam. Indulging in some personal expression. Those dorks you work for would can your ass in a heartbeat if they knew what you'd been up to. Take your boss, Nancarrow, for instance. Now there's a vindictive SOB. He's probably all hot under the collar today because you blew off his daughter's birthday party."

Eric straightened. "How did you know about that? How did you know about the birthday party?"

"It's my *job* to know. And another thing. I know that by the end of today you're going to be out on your keister. Or, at the very least, on the way out. Like I said, they don't care about you. It doesn't matter if you're doing a whiz-bang job of robbing the poor. All that matters to them is image. And if you don't fit that image perfectly, pal, then you're history. The day after they fire you, you won't even be able to get them to take your calls . . . much less get an invite to the Club for pop and weenies. Open your eyes Eric, I'm the only *real* friend you have. That may be pathetic but it's true."

"If it *were* true it certainly *would* be pathetic."

"Get a hold of yourself. Insulting me isn't the answer. Your world is falling apart before your very eyes. Take a close look at your office, this could be the last time you ever see it. When Nancarrow and his chums find out how naughty you've been they're not going to wait for explanations. You'll be standing in the street with your stuff in a cardboard box faster than you can kick an orphan."

"They'll understand it wasn't my fault," he said, not believing it.

"I don't hear any conviction in your voice, Eric."

His vitriol expended, the void it left was rapidly filling with doubt. "You've done this to me. You've ruined my life."

"Eric, if it weren't me it would have been someone else. Your existence is a house of cards. All that's happened is the wind picked up. Don't you understand? You *need* someone like me. I can help. You have to reach out and take something with you when you go. You don't want to be sitting at home next week filling out job applications wishing you had. Think now. Who's going to hire a bank president who was bounced after only a couple months on the job? And the drug charge will taint you even if it doesn't stick. Remember, banks are looking for image, not reality. Eric, you have to understand, this part of your life is over and a new part is about to begin. The question you need to ask yourself now is, would you rather spend the next few years partying in the Caribbean or sitting at home waiting for your assistance check?" There Willie stopped. He'd said it all. Applied the maximum amount of pressure he could muster. Now, as with Moose the day before, he had to shut his mouth.

Eric sat slouched over his desk with trembling hands and a thousand-mile stare. At last, with a halting sigh, he said, "I'll think about it. Call me at 10:30."

Chapter 42

"**D**oreen, when you finish with your customer, lock your drawer and go to Mr. Malette's office, he needs some help with a project."

"All right, Janice. Just give me a minute."

So, here it comes, she thought. He's not even going to do it himself—the coward—he's going to have Andy Malette fire me. Well, that's fine. I'll get out of this dismal bank and find some other job, something interesting, something with a future.

Doreen stamped the savings passbook of the elderly gentleman at her window, wished him a good day, put the CLOSED sign up, locked her drawer, climbed the stairs to the second floor and marched resolutely into Andy Malette's office.

Not waiting for him to speak, she said, "What's the matter, can't he do it himself?"

Malette was taken back by the force of her voice and somewhat confused by the question. "Ah, no. I think he's too busy."

"Too busy to do his own dirty work?"

Malette had been making corrections to a document. He stopped what he was doing and set his pen down. "What dirty work?"

"It's all fine and good if I pick him up and drive him to a bar. But when I get tired of waiting for him to stop making time with that blond ditz and leave, then *I'm* to blame for all his troubles."

"You think *you're* to blame for his troubles?"

"Of course not! But he needs a scapegoat to keep his fragile ego intact, and I guess today's my turn."

Malette was intrigued. "What kind of troubles?"

"Oh, his car breaking down and him missing Ray Nancarrow's daughter's birthday party."

"Oh, gosh! I can see how that might upset him."

Doreen was surprised by his attitude. "So you think what he's doing is okay?"

"What's he doing?"

"Well, he's . . . Aren't you going to . . ." Doreen stopped mid-sentence, then tentatively inquired, "Mr. Malette, why did you call me in here?"

"I asked Janice to send someone in to pull some loan documents. I guess she picked you." A grin was spreading across his face.

"Oh," was all Doreen could muster. Then, "I'd be happy to do that for you."

Malette was working hard to suppress a laugh as he handed her a slip of paper. "Check the files and data base. Pull up everything we have on this guy. He's about to go out of business and we're calling all his loans so we need the stuff pronto. Oh . . . and ah, Doreen, . . . one more thing, just between you and I." Malette leaned forward, looked left then right as if to make sure no one was listening, then whispered, "Never pick up bankers and take them to bars. They'll dump you for the ditz every time."

Doreen's face flushed. "Thanks for the tip."

She made her way back down to the main floor to where the files and records were kept, all the while berating herself for jumping to conclusions. *I guess Willie was right after all,* she mused, shrugging her shoulders. Upon reaching the file cabinets she opened the note. On it was written *Robert Hart,* and under that, *Hart Aviation.*

Chapter 43

About 9:45 Eric got a call from Inspector Hamilton Frank of the Fire Marshall's office. Frank sounded every bit the self-important bureaucrat that he was.

"Mr. Kramer, I'm investigating a fire of suspicious origin which occurred last night at the home of one Orville J. McCullough out on County Road 550."

"What does that have to do with me?"

"Well, it's my understanding, Mr. Kramer, that you got into an altercation with Mr. McCullough last night at the Flat Squirrel bar. Is that correct?"

Oh, Christ! groaned Eric, not more. Is this never going to end? "I don't know any Orville J. McCullough," he said defiantly.

"Well perhaps you know him by his nick-name, Moose? Moose McCullough?"

Eric sighed, rolling his eyes in exasperation. "Yes. Now that you mention it I *did* meet someone named Moose yesterday. I didn't know his last name was McCullough."

"And you got into a fight with him. Is that correct, sir?"

"Ah, no, ah, well no, not really. We had a small misunderstanding, that's all. Really nothing to it."

"Mr. Kramer, I've interviewed several people who were at the Flat Squirrel bar last night and they've made statements to the effect that you made some improper advances toward Mr. McCullough's girlfriend, a Miss Sheila Mackie, whereupon Miss Mackie slapped you, and then Mr. McCullough and yourself got into a fracas which ended up outside. Now, Mr. Kramer, think carefully, would you say this is a fairly accurate representation of what took place?"

"Ahhh . . . not exactly."

"Mr. Kramer, later last evening did you go to Mr.

McCullough's residence with some flammable liquid and light his house on fire?"

The words were like a sucker punch to the gut. "Jesus no!" he cried. "No, of course I didn't light his house on fire. Good God! Why would I do such a thing?"

"Well, Mr. Kramer, you *did* get into a fight with Mr. McCullough, didn't you? And wouldn't that give you some reason to seek revenge?"

"Inspector Frank, let me make this perfectly clear. I did not light Mr. McCullough's house on fire last night. I do not light people's houses on fire. Not last night. Not ever."

"Mr. Kramer, were you at Moose McCullough's house yesterday evening?"

"I've already told you no. No, I was not at Mr. McCullough's house last night. Is that clear?"

"Can you tell me where you were between, say, midnight and two?"

"I was at home sleeping."

"Is there any way for me to verify that, Mr. Kramer?"

"You have my word on it. Isn't that good enough? Isn't the word of a bank president good enough for you?"

"I'm afraid not, sir. Not under these circumstances."

"What circumstances?"

"Mr. Kramer, one of the firemen found what appears to be a personal item of yours at the scene, the presence of which would indicate to me that you were in fact at Mr. McCullough's house at some time in the recent past. Now, would you like to take a moment and think about it? Perhaps you can remember being there within the last few days."

"No. I…was…not…there…"

"One last question, Mr. Kramer. Would you give me the number from your driver's license?"

"Sure, just a moment I . . ." Eric instinctively began reaching toward the left breast pocket of his suit coat where he always carried his wallet, but stopped short. His body went electric with realization and fear. "I . . . I must have left it at home."

"At home, Mr. Kramer?"

"Yes," managed Eric.

"Thank you, Mr. Kramer. That's all the time I'll need from you today. Would it be possible for you to come down and meet with us on, say, Monday morning?

"Yes, I suppose. But I didn't do it."

"Mr. Kramer, I think you should bring your attorney."

Chapter 44

Doreen was still standing in front of the loan files trying to decide what to do when Janice Richards walked up behind her. "Mr. Kramer wants to see you in his office right now." Without speaking, Doreen turned and walked toward Kramer's office.

"You wanted to see me, Mr. Kramer?" she asked, again expecting the worst.

"Yes, Doreen. Come in. Sit down. Make yourself comfortable.

"What a creep," she thought. "Look at that smile. He's taking pleasure in this."

"What do you want?" she said briskly.

To her utter amazement, Eric said, "First, I want to apologize for my poor behavior yesterday. I was rude. There's no excuse for it. And I want you to know how very sorry I am for acting the way I did. Would you accept my apology?"

Doreen was nonplussed, but managed to mumble, "Sure."

"Thank you, Doreen. You don't know how much that means to me."

The first thing that came to her mind was, gee, I guess he had more fun than I thought. "Don't mention it."

Eric shifted around in his chair and wrestled with his thoughts before beginning. "Ah, Doreen, something's come up, and I, ah . . . wonder if you would do me a favor, a very large favor. But, before you answer, I want to say that if you do this I will be deeply in your debt, and I'd do almost anything to repay you."

What could it be, she wondered. What could I possibly do for him that would be so important? "I'm all ears," she said.

"What I'm asking for is this. It seems that some things happened yesterday evening. Things that I didn't know about. Things that I didn't do—wasn't a part of in any way. But . . . ah . . . sometimes it can be very difficult to prove the truth." Eric took a deep breath, exhaled and then went on. "What I need is a person who will say that they know me and that they saw me yesterday evening and will vouch for me. Would you consider doing that for me, Doreen?"

"Well sure, why not? It is the truth. I did see you. I gave you a ride to the Flat Squirrel."

"This whole thing is embarrassing and shameful to me, and it's very hard for me to talk about, but I need to give you the big picture. But before I do, I need your assurance that even if you decide not to help me you won't breathe a word of this conversation to anyone. Would you agree to that?"

"Of course. You didn't rob a bank or anything, did you?"

The words made him wince. "No. Nothing like that."

She waited while he collected himself. This was obviously difficult for him. Finally, Eric began. "Doreen, I'm being accused of a number of crimes."

Her expression went wide so he quickly followed with, "But I didn't do them. Didn't even know about them until today. But, ah, circumstances, circumstances and fate seem to be against me. It seems the police are going to think I did something wrong. And, well, you know how banking is, it's image. And if this stuff gets out, even if later on, when the facts are bought to light, it's proven beyond a shadow of a doubt I wasn't involved, well, that won't matter, it'll be too late for me. I think you can understand that can't you?"

"Mr. Kramer, just what kind of crimes are you talking about?"

"There are several."

"Several? Like a crime spree?" As soon as she saw his face sink she said, "Can I take that back?"

"No, no, you're right. Too right I'm afraid. This morning the police found some marijuana in my BMW. They think it's mine. They think I was smoking pot yesterday when the car broke down. It's going to be in the newspaper for god's sake."

"Wow!"

"Yes, wow. But that's not the half of it. Out there at the Flat Squirrel Bar, well I guess you saw."

"Saw what?"

"You didn't see me get dragged outside by that hulk? I think his name is Moose McCullough."

"No. I left when you were dancing with the blond."

Eric's body went slack at the thought of it. "It was after that. A little after."

"I was gone. I didn't see a thing. Is that what you want me to say?"

"Ah, no, not exactly. You see, some things happened after that. Things I was in no way part of. But I don't have any way to prove it. So here's what I'm asking. Would you consider saying that after that throwback dragged me outside you saw me and drove me home?"

"I suppose I could," she offered.

"And, ah, could you say that I invited you in and you stayed until very late in the evening, say until two o'clock or so?" Then he quickly added, "We were only talking, that's what we'd say. I wouldn't want any one to draw the wrong conclusions, you understand. I mean, I wouldn't want, ah, well, you know."

Doreen thought about where she was last night, about the accident, and Robert, and started to say that she couldn't, but held up as an idea began to form. Instead, she said, "What happened last night that the police think you're involved in?"

Eric sighed, halted, then finally said, "Someone burned down Moose McCullough's house."

"And they think you did it?"

"That's right. Yes, I'm afraid that's exactly right."

With that admission over, Eric sank down in his chair like a man without hope.

"Let me make sure I understand what you're asking.

You want me to say that I stopped to pick you up, and maybe looked inside your car and didn't see or smell any pot, and there was nothing in what you said or the way you acted that would in any way lead me to believe you'd been smoking pot. Would that be about what you'd want me to say?"

Eric brightened. "Yes, yes, that's exactly it."

"And at the bar, I was already outside because we were going to leave and I saw you and that guy come outside and there really wasn't any problem at all, and you walked over and got into the car and we drove around some and went down to the beach for a while then over to your place and talked until late, till about two o'clock, then I went home."

"Oh," said Eric, "if you would say that, it would mean everything to me. I don't know how I could ever repay you, but believe me I'd try. I'd try very hard."

"Let me think about this for a minute, okay?"

"Sure, I understand. I have to use the washroom anyway. Why don't you stay here and make yourself comfortable while I'm gone."

"Thanks," replied Doreen.

Eric left and Doreen sat trying to make sense of it all. Kramer was obviously desperate, desperate enough to ask her, an almost complete stranger, to lie for him. He must be in deep trouble, she thought. Drugs, arson, those are serious crimes. Could he have done it? Or, the better question is, did he do it? Pot. They found pot in his car? I just can't believe he's a pot smoker. Well, it's possible, but it sure doesn't seem likely. And if he were, he'd be the most careful pot smoker in the world. No, I can't believe he'd have pot in his car. And arson. Burning down someone's house? Never. Not even if he were drunk. How in the world did he get in this fix? I imagine if he knew he'd tell me, or he'd tell the police and that would be the end of it. So I guess he doesn't know. He's seeing his career go bye-bye and the only option he has is me. If I lie for him he might be able to get out of this mess. But by asking for my help he's taken a big risk. I could go straight to the police right now and he'd be in deep doo-doo. But how could it work? It's not reasonable to think someone wouldn't remember there was an accident on 550 and that I was in it. Geez. And Mr. Nancarrow, of all people, was there. He must have heard my name. He knows my face. This'll never fly if he's involved. And, the Sheriff's Department has a report. Oh, brother. What am I getting involved in?

Just then Eric poked his head in the door. "Need more time?"

Doreen shook her head. "No, I'm all set."

"What's your decision?"

"I've decided to do it."

Doreen watched Kramer's head go back and his body relax as though he were standing in a rolling surf of joy and a wave of pure relief had just washed over him.

"There are a couple of things we need to clear up," she added.

"What's that?" asked Eric, attentive. "Anything. You say it, I'll do it."

"First, is Mr. Nancarrow going to be in any part of this? I mean, will I have to say this in front of him? Will he know it was me who was with you last night?"

"Nancarrow? Why? I don't understand?"

"Well, I sort of ran into him, briefly, at an accident last night. Oh, I don't think he paid much attention to me. But, if he saw me, I think . . . no, actually I'm sure he'd remember."

Eric mulled it over. "Nancarrow was planning to go back to Chicago on Monday, but now I think he'll be staying on longer. It might be tough, but it's possible we could keep him from finding out. I could tell the police that although you and I are only good friends, our relationship is strictly against bank policy and, for the benefit of both of us keeping our jobs, I can beg them not to disclose your name. That might work."

"And there's something I want?"

"What? Anything. Tell me and I'll do it."

"It's a banking related matter."

"No problem," said Eric, "banking is my life."

"It's about Robert Hart and Hart Aviation."

Eric's joy drained back into the surf. "I'm almost afraid to ask."

"Mr. Malette told me you were going to call in his loans today. I don't want you to do that. That's my condition. That's all I want. It's the only thing I'll ever ask from you."

"But that's Nancarrow's doing. He's in a real dither. I had nothing to do with it. It's all Nancarrow. He's got a bee in his bonnet about Hart losing his license and going out of business. I thought he was going to have a coronary over it this morning. If I don't call Hart's loans he'll fire me on the spot." Eric began to panic, and Willie's words crept into his consciousness.

"I've never been a bank president but I'm smart enough to know that even bank presidents have to take crap from somebody."

"That's my condition, Mr. Kramer. You're asking me to lie for you, risk making a public fool of myself, maybe even go to jail. You're asking an awful lot. And I'm only asking one small thing. Robert Hart is a fine pilot and a wonderful man. He's *not* going out of business. If you check into it you'll see. Nancarrow just hates him because he's is a coward and Robert is a hero. That's the long and short of it."

She paused there, turning her eyes away from Kramer and gazing through one of the ornately trimmed windows which overlooked the city, the harbor and the vastness of Lake Superior. When she turned back, Eric was staring, trancelike, at his desk. He'd loosened his tie, and the top button of his white dress shirt was undone. Although the room was air conditioned, there were beads of sweat on his brow.

"Things happen out of the blue. Things that are totally unanticipated. Things that can't be covered by some plan or insurance policy."

She waited in silence until Eric finally, slowly, looked up, and in a voice that was barely audible said, "I can't."

"What?" replied Doreen, angry. "You ask me to lie for you and take risks that could ruin my life, and you won't even try to help me with this?"

"I can't . . . it just won't work."

The features on Doreen's face hardened. In her clearest and most unequivocal voice she told him, "Yes, Mr. Kramer, it *will* work. You're going to *make* it work. You have two options here. One is that I tell the authorities things that will make them believe that you and I spent the entire evening together. Things that will make them blush and stop asking questions. The other is, I tell them that when I stopped for you I opened the door to your car and smelled marijuana smoke, and I smelled it on your clothes, and your eyes were red, and you were talking about all sorts of crazy things. And, I'll tell them that I left you at the bar because you were making a fool of yourself. And then I'll tell them about our meeting today. Every detail. Now, as I see it, you have two distinct options to choose from. Which is it going to be?"

Eric's head was spinning. He was caught in a vortex of lies and lies to cover up other lies, and he was being sucked down, down from his lofty perch with its antique desk and matching credenza. The floor, with its fine Berber carpet, was becoming concave and things were rolling toward the center. The rich dark oak paneling was bowing inward from the pressure straining to fill the vacuum within the room. Gravity, many times that of the earth, was pulling with tremendous force on the ceiling, pulling it down, down, causing the paneling to compress and splinter. The ceiling was now only a foot or so above his head. A hole had opened in the floor and things were falling into it—into a whirling, howling vortex. He knew where the vortex led. It led to hell. And he was on his way.

Only once in her life had Doreen seen someone who appeared as Eric Kramer did now. It was her mother on the day her father died. But she had her priorities, and Eric Kramer's well-being was way, way down on her list. She would feel sorry for him. That would be okay. But she would not budge an inch on her demand.

Eric finally regained some sense of himself, and in a soft, resigned voice said, "That will be all, Doreen. Thank you for coming in. I'll try to think this thing through and . . .

and find a solution that will please you." It was a lie. He knew it was a lie when he said it. But he couldn't have her leave thinking he wasn't going to try. God only knew what she might do. She could walk out into the lobby and start screaming rape and the charge would simply and without further question be added to the tally on his rap sheet.

When she was gone, Eric sat alone in his office and thought. But to no avail. In the past, reason had always worked for him and kept him safe. But it did not work now. For he no longer lived in a world of reason. Two plus two still equaled something, but that something was three and a half, or four and five-eighths, or the square root of a hackmatack multiplied by its age in dog years. There was no way out. It was a Hobson's choice—no choice at all. He'd fought the good fight, but it was over. He would be out by Monday . . . Tuesday at the latest. He'd be disgraced. Sullied goods. No one would want him.

Then the thought began from within and rose like a fast tide under a heavy moon.

"and the folks you work for say 'Gee Eric, we'd like to keep you on, but you know . . .', and you use up all your savings and lose your home and you're out on the street in the winter with no money and no job and no friends and no place to go, all because of some purely chance occurrence. Don't you think it would be nice to have a little nest egg tucked away for just such an event?"

The money! He could take some with him. He wouldn't have to live like a pauper, begging and scraping. Then he said aloud, "And maybe, just maybe, if I do it right I can have the money *and* keep my job. The evidence of a bomb would explain everything. It's the *only* way to explain everything. And, either way, I'll keep the money. Or at least half."

Chapter 45

"Where have you been?" complained Eric when he found it was the controller on the phone. "It's nearly eleven o'clock. Don't you have a watch?"

"Of course I have a watch, limp-wrist. But I don't let it rule my life."

"It would have been a lot better if you'd have called me at home this morning. It's . . . it's hard to talk here."

"What's the matter? Do you share a phone?"

"Of course not. But my secretary puts these calls through; she knows we've been talking."

"What? You're not allowed to talk to people? Think of me as a customer looking to take out a loan. A very large loan."

"You don't get it. You think the police aren't smart. They *are* smart. And if money comes up missing they're going to be prying into everything, and that probably means phone records too. Or isn't that something you're concerned with? I know it's something *I'm* concerned with. Details. Details are important."

"Look, chumly, I know details are important. Details are my life."

"I thought you said bombs were your life?"

"Yeah, bombs and details, my life revolves around both."

"I'll bet it does."

"It does. So listen. What I want you to do is go to the pay phone at the Shell station on the corner of Washington and Fourth. I'll call you and we can talk. Be there in ten minutes. Got that?"

"Yes, yes, I have it. But I still think you should've called me at home."

"Well, the next time I call for a date I promise to call you at home. And I'll send flowers too. But this time I didn't and I'm really, really sorry. I'll never do it again. Is that enough? Are you satisfied?"

"Okay. All right. But it just makes me worry about your planning. You do have this thing all planned out, don't you? You do have a plan?"

"A plan? Of course I have a plan. Plans are my life"

"I wish you hadn't said that."

"Be there."

"All right."

Chapter 46

The pay phone at the Shell station rang and Eric picked it up. "Hello?
"Hello."
"Who's this?"
"The Avon lady you nimrod. Who do you think it is?"
"I just wanted to be sure."
"Okay, now listen carefully. Go down behind the Snowline Theater, you'll find a garbage can there. The belt is in the can. Put it on underneath your suit coat. Then go back to your office and call Mattson's. Tell them to bring a loaner car over for you on the double. A big one too. Got it?"
"Yes."
"Now, I need some information from you."
"What?"
"Who usually closes the vault and locks up? Who's usually the last person in the bank? When does the guard leave?"
"Most of the employees leave soon after we close at twelve. The guard unlocks the door, lets them out, then locks it again. A few employees have to stay to finish the counts and reconciliations. The guard stays during that time. When the reconciliation is done and everything that's going into the vault is in, Andy Malette, the vice president, usually closes and locks it, then calls the alarm company to tell them it's set. After that everyone who's still around leaves in a group with the guard."
Willie pondered the information, then said, "Here's what you do. Send Malette away on some errand. Far enough so he won't be coming back to the bank to close up. Tell the employees you'll be closing today. When the time comes and all the money's in the vault, tell the employees there's something you need to do before closing the vault, maybe

some paperwork, so they should all go ahead and leave and not wait for you and waste their beautiful Saturday afternoon standing around in some shit-hole bank."

"Are those the words you think I should use? Shit-hole bank?"

"Use your own discretion as to adjectives, but get everyone to leave."

"Okay. It'll be tricky. It's strictly against policy. But I can make something up and bully everyone into leaving. What then?"

"Put the money from the vault into those big sacks you use and drag them over by the front door."

"Okay. Then what?"

"Then go get the car, pull it around front by the door, load the bags in and drive away."

"*That's* your plan?"

"Yeah. What's wrong with it?"

"Well, gosh, I don't know. Maybe it's just that there are dozens of people walking the streets at noon on an average Saturday and they might think it's a teensy bit odd that a lone man is loading huge bags of money into the trunk a rental car in front of a closed bank. You don't need to be a Rhodes Scholar to know that that's a bank robbery in progress."

"I suppose you've got a better idea?"

"Well, what's your back-up plan?"

"What back-up plan?"

"You don't have a back-up plan? That's it? Drag the bags out the front door, pile them in a car and drive away? I might as well sing a few choruses of Jailhouse Rock while I'm at it, because that's where I'm going to be about ten minutes after I start."

"What do you mean? You're the president of the bank. You're allowed to do stuff like that."

"I am not."

"You are if you have a bomb wrapped around you."

"Hmm . . . You make a good point."

"So you'll do it?"

Eric hesitated. "Don't you have some other ideas? Something more subtle?"

"Is there a back door?"

"The back door is alarmed. It's only used in emergencies. If the door is opened the alarm goes off. The police will be there in two minutes or less. It's been timed."

"That won't work."

"No kidding. Any other ideas?"

"How about a window?"

"The only windows that open are on the second floor."

"So?"

"I'd have to carry the bags up to the second floor."

"So?"

"Those bags are going to be heavy."

"Are you telling me your building isn't ADA compliant? Don't you have an elevator?"

"Yes. Well . . . I guess I could use the elevator to bring them up."

"See."

"Then what?"

"First, park the car in the alley behind the bank. Then throw the bags out the window behind the car. Then go out and load the bags into the trunk. Then drive off."

"I guess it could work. I could have the window open before noon comes and the alarm company does their check. I could tell them that it's closed and they can ignore the light or whatever that tells them it's open. I could have the car there ready to go, shoo all the employees out of the bank, fill up the bags in the vault, drag them to the elevator, drag them out on the second floor and over to Andy Malette's office—that's the one with the window on the alley—toss them out behind the car, close the vault, call the alarm company, lock up the bank, go into the alley, load up the bags and drive off. How does that sound?"

"Pretty good, amigo. But I think you should omit a couple of steps."

"Which ones?"

"Well, after you toss the bags, just get the hell out of

there, load up and drive off. You see, we criminals don't care if the vault is set or the front door is wide open, all we care about is getting the money in the car and getting away as fast as possible. All those extra steps take time. Time is the enemy here. *Comprende?*"

"Yes. Good point. I'm being forced to do this so I can't take the time to lock up. Right?"

"Right."

No one spoke for a while. Willie broke the silence. "How much money do you think is there?"

"I don't know for sure, but I'd guess about six million."

Willie tried to stay calm. "I guess that's enough."

"Yes, it'll be fine. Three million apiece."

"What? You want three million?"

"That's right. I want half."

"That's too much."

"I'm certainly doing half the work or more, so I want half the money and not a penny less."

"But . . . but . . . there are other people involved."

"Who?"

"I can't tell you who. But they're going to want to get paid. And if they don't they're gonna be pissed. Thirds, that's the best I can do. You keep a third, I'll keep a third, a third goes to the others."

"Do these other people know I'm involved?"

"No. They're not that close to the action."

"Good. Let's keep it that way."

"That's fine with me. They've played other roles. They're not even in town right now. But they know who *I* am. And if I don't pay them they'll come and take it from me in a very unpleasant way. So I'm kind of between a rock and a hard place on this. You can understand that, can't you?"

"Ah . . . yes . . . I guess so. Well, okay, thirds."

"All right, it's a plan. You'd better get going. Remember, you've got to call Mattson's and get that car. If they can't get one over to you, call a rental company and have them bring one."

"Okay. . . . One last thing."

"Somehow I knew there would be."

"Where do I drive after I load up the money?"

"I'll call you on the Bat radio and give you instructions."

"Well okay. Here goes."

Eric walked behind the theater and found the garbage can. The belt was under some old newspapers. He wrapped it around his waist under his suit coat and tried to buckle it, but the tongue wouldn't slide all the way into the latch.

He spoke toward the belt. "The buckle doesn't work."

Out of the speaker came, "Push on it!"

"I *am* pushing on it, you hemorrhoid! It won't buckle. The darn thing's broken."

"You'll have to improvise."

"What are you talking about *improvise*?"

"Hold the buckle closed with one hand so it *looks* like it's buckled."

"Just exactly who am I trying to fool?"

"Just do it. Just in case. Now get going, we don't have time to argue."

"All right, mister details, I'll get going, but only because we're getting short on time. You should have done a better job of building this thing. You know, if you'd taken more care in the beginning, problems like this wouldn't occur."

"Judas Priest! Get going before I have an aneurysm."

"Okay."

"All right."

Chapter 47

Eric skulked back to the bank with his hand in his bulging coat, looking as though he'd just eaten the entire smorgasbord at Bonanza and had a crippling stomach ache. He walked straight to his office, called Mattson, and told him unless he wanted to see a convoy of tow trucks headed his way to repossess every last goddamned car on his lot, he'd better have a new Cadillac loaner parked in the President's spot at the bank, with the keys in it, within fifteen minutes. He then called Malette and told him to go out to Hart Aviation and inventory every last damn thing in the place. "This is straight from Nancarrow," he added for emphasis.

At 11:50 Eric walked to a window that overlooked the parking lot and saw to his satisfaction that a new, lime-green Cadillac was parked in his spot. While doing it, his grip on the buckle loosened and he ended up standing at the window with the belt dangling from his hand in front of him. Exasperated, he quickly balled it up, tucked it under his coat and scurried back to his office. Then, with the door closed, he sat on the edge of his desk, wrapped the belt back around his midriff and used about twenty pieces of Scotch tape to hold the buckle in a semi-fastened position.

At 11:55 he called his secretary and told her to advise the staff that Andy Malette had to leave on business and that he would be locking up. The bank closed precisely at twelve. The guard ushered out the last customers and locked the door from the inside. The count and reconciliation proceeded as usual. Most of the employees, including Doreen Harmon, finished their chores and left.

About ten minutes later, Janice called up to his office and told him everything was done and the vault was ready to be closed. Eric was sweating like a penguin in a steam bath as he shuffled downstairs to face the assembled employees.

"Janice, you and the others can go now. I have a few details to take care of here, then I'll lock up."

"What is it, Mr. Kramer? I'd be glad to help," offered Janice.

"It's ah . . . some technical stuff. I have to do it myself. Thanks anyway, but you can go."

"Really, Mr. Kramer, I'd be glad to help."

By then the other six or so remaining employees were watching the transaction between Kramer and the head teller with interest."

"I told you, it's technical. I have to do it myself."

"But . . . you know the rules, sir. We're not supposed to leave unless we all leave together."

Eric gave her a look that could have chilled a nuclear plasma fire. Then, with a voice that began softly but gained in fury as he spoke, he said, "Janice, I don't think it's at all fair that you and the other employees should have to spend one more minute of this beautiful Saturday afternoon standing around in some shit-hole bank—*do you?*"

Janice's mouth fell open, and the other employees took a collective step backward. Then they turned and made for the door as quickly as decorum would allow. Janice hot on their heels.

After the last person was out, Eric used his key to lock the door from the inside. He smiled and gave a two-fingered salute to the aging guard who tipped his hat and strolled away with the others.

Eric was now alone. He proceeded directly to the vault and began loading everything of value into large bank sacks stamped with the First Northern National name and logo. At first he did it carefully, but as the minutes dragged on and his internal pressure increased he began grabbing armfuls of bills and anything else on the shelves; dumping them willy-nilly into the bags. When he finally stopped there were eight full bags. Eric lugged the bags to the elevator and lorried them to the second floor. Then he dragged them into

Malette's office and over to the window, opened it, stuck his head out to make sure the alley was clear, then panicked when he realized he hadn't moved the car.

"I don't have the car," shouted Eric toward his waist.

"What?" came the crackling reply.

"I don't have the car. I forgot to move the car."

"Can't you do anything right?"

"Listen, there's no time for that. Any minute now the alarm company will call and ask why the vault isn't closed and why we haven't called them. And regardless of what I tell them, if it's not closed by 12:30 they have instructions to call the police as a precaution. Then the police will come here and check up on things. It's 12:23 right now. I don't have time to go out and get the car from the lot, drive it around the block into the alley, then come back up here and throw the bags out, then go down and load them and drive away, all in seven minutes. You've got to get the car and drive it into the alley. I'll start throwing the bags out now. When I'm done I'll lock the vault and call the alarm company. That'll give us more time. But you've got to get that car into the alley, otherwise someone might see the bags lying there and get suspicious. Understand?"

"You're dumber than a bag of hammers. I can't believe you forgot the car."

"Hey, listen. While you were out there lolling around some phone booth pounding your pud, I was in here working like a dog, and taking all the risks too. So get your ass going and get that car. It's a lime-green Cadillac. The keys are in the ignition."

"You had them leave the keys in the ignition? Is that safe?"

"Get moving, you moron, before I blow myself up out of spite!"

Eric began muscling the heavy bags of money out of Malette's office window. Hearing them land with a *woomph* on the concrete below. After the eighth bag was through he looked out and saw them in a random pile twenty feet below. Then he heard a car and realized with relief it was a lime-green Cadillac backing up the alley.

Eric checked his watch. It was 12:27. He raced out of Malette's office and down the hall, took the stairs four steps at a time, sprinted to the vault, slammed it shut and spun the lock. As he did so, the Scotch tape gave out and the belt fell from his waist to the floor. With no time to spare, Eric scooped up the belt and ran up the stairs to Malette's office. Tossing the belt on the desk, he frantically spun the Rolo-dex until he found the number for United Alarm Service. He dialed, then took a breath and tried to sound as normal as possible.

"Hi. This is Eric Kramer at First Northern National, customer code 1311972. We had some late transactions here, but we're all finished now. I'm calling to tell you the vault is closed and locked and you can set the alarm."

"Mr. Kramer, we're getting an open window light on the second floor of your building."

"Oh, gosh, silly me. I opened a window earlier to get a breath of fresh air. I must have forgotten to close it. If you'll hold on I'll close it now and you can check to see that the light goes off."

"Sure, fine, sir. But it's twelve twenty-nine and if it's not closed in about 30 seconds our computer's going to automatically call the police."

Tension gripped Eric like a giant squid. "No problem. I understand. I'll take care of it right now."

He put down the receiver and raced to the window to close it—noting with satisfaction that only two bags remained to be loaded into the Cadillac. He pulled the window shut and dashed back to the phone.

"All closed," he said.

"Yeah, ah, Mr. Kramer, looks like the light is out now. Okay, you have a good afternoon."

"You too. Bye."

With that over Eric relaxed and even allowed himself a

slight smile. The smile had been on his face for exactly one nanosecond when he realized his mistake.

"*NO-O-O-O-O-O,*" he screamed. Bounding to the window, he pressed his face on the glass to get a view of the alley below. It was empty.

Chapter 48

W illie couldn't believe his good fortune. He was in a Cadillac loaded to the brim with eight huge bags packed with money. All his dreams of avarice combined paled in comparison to this windfall. Driving as carefully as a student on exam day, he pulled out of the alley and turned west on Front Street. He traveled as far as Fourth, turned north, then worked his way through town to where Wright Street intersects County Road 550. Then he headed north on 550 at the maximum posted speed, only slowing when he saw the turnoff to Harlow Lake. There were no other cars in sight as he swung onto the dusty gravel of the Harlow Lake Road. Confident, now that he was on his home turf, Willie dug a victory joint out of the pocket of his worn flannel shirt, lit it, and had his first taste of the good life. He drove up the road seeing nothing of consequence, save one old Chevy Nova parked in a spot generally used by fishermen. Its owner was not in sight.

When Willie arrived at the cabin, he turned the car around and parked. Then, in full hustle mode, ran to the cabin, unlocked the door, went in, grabbed a handful of plastic garbage bags, shoved them in his pocket, then ran out to the shed where he kept his garbage. A few minutes later found him lumbering to the Cadillac under the weight of two plastic bags filled with old newspapers he'd collected for starting fires in the woodstove. After depositing them in the backseat, he scooted back to the cabin, locked up, jogged back to the Caddy, cranked it up and raced back down the bumpy road toward Harlow Lake.

Skidding to a halt when he reached the abandoned Marquette and Huron Mountain railroad tracks, he punched the trip counter, spun the wheel to the left and began motoring directly up the railroad right of way. With the wide wheelbase of the Caddy and the wheels straddling the tracks, the tracks provided directional guidance, allowing Willie to take his hands off the steering wheel. With nothing to do but enjoy the ride, Willie relit his joint, rolled down the window and bounced his way over the railroad ties toward Big Bay. When the trip counter was nearing two miles he became alert, finally stopping at a place where a galvanized metal culvert about four feet in diameter traversed beneath the tracks. The culvert drained a swampy area to the west. But it was late summer and, as Willie already knew, the flowage was dry.

He got out, scrambled down the grade to the culvert, inspected it and climbed back up to the Caddy. Then he opened the trunk and back doors and heaved the bank sacks and bags of newspapers, down the grade toward the opening of the culvert. That done, he went back down the grade again.

After opening one of the sacks to reassure himself it actually contained money, Willie shoved six of them deep into the culvert. He then transferred the contents of the remaining two bank sacks into several fresh garbage bags. When that was done, he packed the empty bank sacks about three-quarters full with bags of newspapers. After that he sifted through the garbage bags of money, pulling out the small bills and placing a thick layer of them on top of the bags of newspaper in the bank sacks. Last, he stowed the garbage bags containing money in the culvert with the rest of the bank sacks. Then he took care to place some brush inside the opening of the culvert so that, in the extremely unlikely event that someone were to look inside, all they would see was brush and darkness.

He hauled the two garbage-dummied bank sacks back up the grade, locking them in the trunk of the Caddy. Then scrambled down the grade to the opposite end of the culvert, filled that end with brush, then climbed back up to the car again.

With everything secure, Willie brushed away his footprints, got back in the Caddy, started up, dropped it into reverse and cheerfully bounced his way back to the Harlow Lake crossing. From there he cautiously motored back to town and—making sure there was no one around when he did it—parked the car three blocks from where Eric Kramer lived. Then he nonchalantly ambled downtown to where he'd left his Ford.

One last detail, he thought. The belt.

Chapter 49

Kramer ran out of Malette's office, down the hall, down the stairs, across the lobby to the front doors, fumbled with his keys, unlocked the door and stepped outside into the sunlight. Nothing. There was no Cadillac in sight. He noticed people beginning to stare at him so he retreated into the bank and relocked the door. Moving several feet to the side so no one could see him through the glass doors, he sank down on his haunches and began pounding his fist against the polished marble floor.

"How stupid. How incredibly stupid of me." Tears of anger welling in his eyes. "How could I have done that? How could I have let him go with all the money? Now that he has it my leverage is gone and I'll never hear from him again." He was totally beside himself and began hyperventilating so badly he had to put a trembling hand over his mouth to stop from passing out.

After several minutes the shaking subsided, and Eric slowly arose. There was nothing to do now but lock up and go home. "At least I have the belt," he sighed, "at least I have the proof that it wasn't my fault."

But, even with that in mind, it was not enough. For Eric Kramer had crossed some invisible threshold. He was no longer Eric Kramer the hard-working, responsible banker—and although he didn't know it, never would be again. He'd done the forbidden. And in taking what he'd never before even coveted, had tasted the feeling of freedom, sweet freedom. He could no more go back to his old way of being than a new mother could reclaim her virginity.

Eric roamed though the bank until he found a plastic shopping bag. He dropped the belt into the bag, locked up the bank and walked home. Arriving, he did another thing he'd never done before—filled a glass with ice, filled the space around it full with Glenlivet scotch, and began drinking at one in the afternoon.

Shuffling into his living room, he collapsed into his favorite chair, dumped the belt out onto the ottoman and sat there staring at it. Although he didn't believe it would happen, there was always a chance, a slim chance, that the controller would contact him again to retrieve it. He tried his best to think of anything that could help him, but his glands had pumped so much adrenalin into his system during the previous five hours that thinking was chemically impossible, so he sat there with the shades drawn and in the semidarkness sipped his scotch and waited.

Chapter 50

Nearly two hours went by before the phone rang. Eric reached out and picked up the receiver. "Hello?"

"Hello. Glad to see you're home."

Eric didn't say anything.

"Well, sport, ready to finish this thing up?"

"Yes. Yes, of course," he answered, spirits soaring.

"Okay then. Take US-41 toward Negaunee and take a right on 510, you know, the back way to Big—"

"Yes, yes I know. What then?"

"Up about three miles is a metal-girder bridge that spans the Nash River. Do you know where that is?"

"Yes, of course."

"On the far side of the bridge there's a dirt road to the left. It goes to an access site on the river."

"Okay."

"Drive down there and wait in the car. I'll contact you."

"I don't have a car."

"Oh yeah. I almost forgot. The Caddy's on the corner of Second and Hewitt. That's about three blocks from—"

"I know where it is," interrupted Eric. "I live here you know."

"Of course, of course. Just checking. Details you understand."

"Sure. Ahh . . . I don't suppose the money's still in the car?"

"Right. And I spray painted my name and address on the windshield so you could bring me my share."

"I didn't think so."

"Okay. Let's get moving, lead butt. Time's a wastin'. If you're not there in twenty minutes I'll assume don't want to trade that fine belt for these two big sacks of money."

"Don't worry, I'll be there. Just one last thing."

"Somehow I knew there would be."

"You *are* going to blow the belt up, aren't you? I mean, you're not going to take it with you? I *need* you to blow it up so I'll have proof there really was a bomb."

"Of course I'll blow it up. That's what I said I'd do, didn't I? I can't leave the dang thing hanging around. Come on out to the bridge; we'll make the swap. Then I'll blow the belt up and we'll both be on our merry way."

"I'll be there in twenty minutes."

"All right."

"Okay."

Eric grabbed the bag and tossed the belt back into it. He ran out the door without locking up and hurried to where the controller told him the Caddy was parked. It was there. He got in, found the keys in the ignition, started up and broke all of the basic speed laws driving to the Nash River Bridge. After finding the turnoff, he parked in the area the controller told him about, then sat in the car and waited. He didn't have long to wait.

"What took you?" said the voice from the belt.

"What do you mean? I got here as fast as I could," replied Eric toward the bag on the front seat.

"You drive like old people screw."

"Enough already. Let's get this over with. I have a lot left to do today . . . like go to the police station and tell them I've been forced to rob my own bank. It's not going to be easy. And I'd like some quality time for myself too."

"Yes, yes, of course. Well, let's get to it. Listen now, here's the serious part. Strange as it may seem, I've kind of gotten to like you, and it would take a chunk of fun out of my day if I were to have to blow you up. So don't screw around or get any funny ideas."

"Fine."

"I'm going to show you the money first so you'll know it's there and you have it. Then you're going to bring the belt up on the bridge. After that, when I tell you to, you're going to throw it off the bridge into the water. Then you have to lie down on the road bed while I blow it up. Do you understand?"

"Hey, I don't want to get blown up too."

"You won't. There's not that much explosive in it. And the concrete and pavement of the road bed on the bridge will protect you."

"Okay, let's do it. Where's the money?"

"It's in the trunk."

"You're joking?"

"Nope. See for yourself."

Eric got out of the Caddy, went around back and opened the trunk. There they were, two huge bank sacks.

"Hey, wait a minute. There are only two bags in here. I'm supposed to get a third."

"Don't worry," said Willie, "I packed in extra so you'd get your fair share."

Being the cautious type, Eric undid the clasp that held the top rope of one of the sacks, stretched the mouth open, pulled out the flap and watched as cash spilled onto the floor of the trunk. With a satisfied nod he shoved the money back in the sack, refastened the clasp and slammed the trunk shut. Then he hurried back around the car, reached in and snatched the belt out of the plastic bag and then ran up the access road and out onto the bridge.

"Go to the center," commanded Willie.

"Okay," said Eric.

"Hold the belt out over the edge of the railing. Over the water."

"All right."

"On the count of three let go of the belt and drop to the pavement as if your life depends on it, because it does."

"I've got it. I've got it. Let's just get this thing over with."

Willie began counting. "One . . .two . . .three . . ."

On three, Eric let go of the belt and dropped to the pavement. Willie saw him lie down and pushed the button on the garage door opener. The explosion was deafening. The bridge rocked. Eric thought his eardrums would burst. Then it was over.

Eric scrambled to his feet and surveyed the water below. He couldn't see any trace of the belt. But there must be, he reasoned. And people must have heard the explosion. I've got to get out of here, hide the money, then get to the police as fast as I can so they can confirm the existence of the bomb. And that's what he did.

Chapter 51

By the time Eric got back to the Cadillac, Willie and the green Ford were already moving at top speed toward US-41 and the anonymity its volume of traffic would provide. He reasoned that once he got into the traffic it would be all over except the party. And he was right. Nothing of consequence happened on his way through town or back to his cabin. But the day's work wasn't over yet. He knew he had some details to take care of. And he found it interesting to think that he'd become quite a bit more detail oriented within the past twenty-four hours.

Willie found an old shopping bag and placed in it every piece of material from of his workshop that could possibly be traced to the fragments of the bomb, including the plans and diagrams in his notebook. He took the bag of remnants, as well as the remote control slash radio slash receiver device and the handgun he'd stolen but fortunately never had to use, and a round-point shovel, along with two beers and a fresh joint, and walked a half-mile into the woods, to a place where no one would ever find them. He dug a three foot deep hole in the middle of a copse of cedars, dropped the bag of scrap in, tossed the gun on top, stomped the stuff down with his foot, then refilled the hole with dirt, stomped it again, and refurbished the surface to its original condition. After that he walked most of the way back to the cabin before stopping to take sustenance and revel in his glory. He knew the cops would never find the remote control or the parts. He doubted *he* could find them again. The bomb was gone, the money was safe, and he hadn't been seen. And, with the exception of Carmen, no one on the planet knew he was involved. It was the perfect crime.

Chapter 52

From the exchange point at the Nash River Bridge, Eric drove straight home, hiding the sacks of money in the only place he could think of at the time—his basement. He then drove directly to the police station and spent nearly three hours going over every detail of the events of the previous twenty-four hours. There were omissions, fabrications and other significant story adjustments of course, all of which helped to place him in a more favorable light vis-à-vis the incident at the Flat Squirrel, his conversation with Doreen Harmon and the actual extent of his participation in the theft. Lucky for Eric, he had a good memory. For, as it happened, this was the first of many such questionings by the police, insurance investigators and even the FBI.

All in all, the episode ended with Eric's reputation for the most part intact—at least as far as the police and public were concerned. Unfortunately, Ray Nancarrow and the board of directors of the First Northern National Bank were not as understanding as they might have been. They urged Eric to take a one month paid vacation "for health reasons" and then to resign "to pursue other opportunities." Thus giving him the opportunity to leave with a semblance of dignity, rather than being summarily ejected on his can.

Actually this wasn't so bad considering Eric was already divorced from the idea of ever being a banker again. He was totally pumped for millionaire mode. So much so that he'd found it extremely difficult to play the role of victim during the police interview. It was acting at its finest, he thought, but he wouldn't be an actor for long.

After three hours of police grilling, Eric was finally allowed to leave the station. He took a taxi home, showered, ate dinner and then took a calculated walk around the neighborhood to make sure he wasn't being watched.

Satisfied no strange eyes were about, he returned home. Then, after locking and bolting the door, and breathless with anticipation, he made for the basement to inventory the contents of the sacks. It wasn't long after he'd opened the first one and reached deep inside that his euphoria imploded like a marshmallow universe. The sack had been dummied. Checking the second one, he found it to be the same. The controller had made a fool of him. He quickly tallied the small amount of cash Willie'd used as fools bait to make the deception work. His portion of the booty amounted to a measly $17,136 in small bills and dozens of moldy newspapers. Leaving the cash and everything else lying helter-skelter on the basement floor, Eric climbed the steps, turned off the light and stood like a zombie in the middle of his kitchen as the enormity of his situation descended upon him. Then, writhing in anguish, he sought succor from his liquor cabinet. But even a full bottle of high-quality scotch could not begin to heal the deep psychic wound that Willie's treachery had inflicted.

Chapter 53

Willie, too, was in for an unpleasant surprise. He stayed at the cabin for the rest of the weekend and resumed his normal erratic work-schedule the following Monday. He'd called Carmen Saturday after he'd stashed the loot and they'd agreed to lay low for a week, then to meet at his cabin the following Friday to decide how to proceed.

Earlier and more conservative thinking aside, Willie desperately wanted the two of them to take the cash and blow town at once in the green Ford—irrespective of the unfavorable impression it may leave on those charged with retrieving the stolen property. Carmen, on the other hand, being the practical sort she was, urged caution.

"Willie," she'd said over and over again, "we don't want people following us around and trying to hunt us down. The only way they'll ever suspect us is if we stop our normal routine and disappear. We can leave later. People are always moving here and there. After things cool down it won't seem out of the ordinary for us to leave town. But not now. It would point the finger of blame right at us. Willie, I love you. You're the most wonderful, brilliant, handsome, sexy, exciting man I've ever known. I want to spend the rest of my life enjoying you, and us, and the good life—not looking over my shoulder worrying about the police. Please, Willie. I know it's hard, but please, let's stay here for a little while. Six months would be best, a couple months at least, or even a few weeks, a few weeks might be enough." And, in the end, Willie thought Carmen was probably right. It wouldn't be the perfect crime if insurance detectives or whatever were chasing them all over the world. So he relented and agreed to stay for a few weeks.

The next Friday came and went with no Carmen knocking on his cabin door. Saturday, too, drifted by with no beautiful, dark-haired visitor. By Sunday noon Willie had reached his breaking point and drove the twenty-five miles to the Hodges residence. But when he cruised by the house he noticed the white jeep was missing. What to do? So he drove into town, found a pay phone and dialed her number. Dick Hodges answered, but Willie was prepared.

"Hi, Mr. Hodges. My name is Jim Velasquez and I'm a second cousin of Carmen's. I live out in California, but I'm here in Northern Michigan on business and thought I'd give her a call to say hello. Is she in?"

"Well, Mr. Velasquez, I'm afraid you're a little late."

"Late? In what way, sir?"

"Ah . . . you see, Carmen and I haven't been getting along so well lately, and I'm afraid things came to a head last Sunday and . . . er . . . well . . . she left."

"She left?" said Willie weakly.

"That's right. She packed a suitcase, said good-bye and drove off. Said she needed some time to think. Said she'd call me in a couple of days to talk about things. But she hasn't, and I really don't expect she will. We had, well . . . a rather large age difference between us and I guess we both knew it wasn't working out. That's the way these things go sometimes. Anyway, if you see her, tell her I wish her all the best."

"Sure," said Willie, lost in thought, "sure." She was gone. And she hadn't even said good-bye. He couldn't believe it.

He drove around aimlessly for an hour, then headed back toward the cabin. Along the way an ugly thought crept into his mind. He tried to dismiss it, but it wouldn't go. So when he got to the railroad crossing on the Harlow Lake Road, he turned up the tracks and bounced his way to where the fortune was hidden.

Upon arriving he half leaped, half slid down the grade to the opening of the culvert. Falling to his knees, he peered inside. Then his face went slack, mouth fell open and barbed thorns of misery penetrated to the very core of every cell in his mind and body. The brush had been pulled out. The bank sacks were gone. Then he noticed a manila envelope tucked under a cairn of stones and pulled it out. Opening it, he found $3,000 in small bills and a note.

> *Dear Willie,*
> *I know this must be a shock to you, but I can't help it. It's all for the best.*
> *Love, Carmen*

Willie sank into a miasma of alcohol-fueled despair which lasted for months. Then, when the cash ran low, he reluctantly resumed his normal business activities. But other than an occasional excursion to the Squirrel for a bout of drinking, he completely receded from any social contact whatsoever.

*   *   *

Eric, too, withdrew. But, unlike Willie, Eric had a mission; his own, personal holy war to find and reclaim what, in his mind, was rightfully his. He became totally obsessed with every minor detail of the events that surrounded the heist. Immersing himself in research, he gathering a huge database and spent endless hours sifting through leads and possibilities. The lack of clues was frustrating, but his methodical mind concentrated on those that he had. And he vowed he would not be denied.

His few friends abandoned him, including Annie, who upon hearing of his disgrace never mentioned his name again. His meticulous personal grooming habits went by the wayside. His hair grew long, and the color began to darken. At first the change was simply from lack of sunlight. But later, when Eric understood that disguise would be to his advantage, he used dye to change it to dark brown. He lost weight, and his once athletic body became gaunt. His formerly smooth, tanned face became sunken and sallow. He took to dressing in second-hand workman's clothing which, from time to time, he slept in. He stopped shaving. And, in public, he kept his eyes hidden behind dark sunglasses. When the change was complete, people he'd known all his life would pass him by without hint of recognition.

In addition, he took to roaming the streets at all hours and frequenting roadside establishments, such as the Flat Squirrel—sitting in darkened corners, surreptitiously watching other patrons and scribbling notes in a tattered binder.

Over time, his persistence began to pay off.

Chapter 54

It was exactly seven months and three weeks after the theft. The long Northern Michigan winter was nearly over when Willie brushed the snow off the old, green Ford, loaded it with repaired amps and headed into town for a delivery to Bonello's and to refurbish his dwindling supplies. While in town, among other things, Willie checked his post office box, balled up the assorted contents—mostly advertisements and solicitations—and tossed them pell-mell on the seat of the Ford for future reference. Later that afternoon, back at the cabin and having nothing to do, he trudged out to the truck and retrieved the stuff, bringing it in and dumping it on the kitchen table. Then he sifted through it, hoping to find something of at least marginal interest to dull the effect of a serious bout of cabin fever. About three-quarters of the way through the pile he found a letter addressed to Dr. Willie Salo. His usual habit was to summarily toss such an obviously mislabeled document—which would almost certainly be a request for money—directly into the mouth of the pot-bellied wood stove he used for heat. But something about the writing on the envelope caused him to pause. It was addressed in longhand. Groups pandering for money virtually never wrote things out by hand. What the heck, he thought, ripping the end off the envelope and dumping its contents on an uncluttered portion of the table. What he saw lying there came as an enormous surprise. It was a photograph of a tropical beach. On the beach was a deck chair and an end table. On the table was a drink with an umbrella in it. And on the arm of the chair hung a skimpy yellow Speedo. He turned the picture over. On the back, in flowing script, was written,

Dear Doctor,

I have a problem that needs immediate medical attention and was wondering if you could prescribe a course of treatment.

Get a room at the Blue Coral Motel. It's on the beach. I'll find you.

P.S. Clothing optional.

The envelope also contained an open airline ticket to the island of Aruba.

Willie was ecstatic. He quickly made what small preparations were necessary to close up the cabin, packed a few items of clothing in an old suitcase and drove through Marquette to the airport.

When he got to the ticket counter he was in luck, there were still three seats available on the next departure. He immediately booked one of them and checked his luggage with the agent. As it turned out, flight time was still several hours away. Not wanting to hang around the small terminal building, Willie rambled back into town and stopped at a new bar Big Jim had opened there called The Nut Shell.

The bar was dimly lit and moody, a marked contrast to the happy-go-lucky atmosphere of the Squirrel. There were about a dozen mid-afternoon patrons scattered about the place, mostly in pairs, with one or two tucked away in corners for reasons of their own.

Willie glad-handed Big Jim, laughed, told jokes and stories, filled the jukebox with quarters, danced with the barmaid, downed several beers and, much to Jim's amazement, even bought two rounds for the crowd. Then, with his departure time fast approaching, Willie bid farewell to the patrons, drove to the airport, deposited the Ford in long-term parking and waited for his flight to board.

Marquette had recently acquired major jet service to the Chicago hub and Willie found the window seat in the new MD-80 to be more comfortable than he would have imagined, but less roomy than he would have preferred. As the plane filled, he found himself hoping no one would sit next to him and impinge upon his elbowroom. But the flight was now booked to capacity, and in the end the seat was taken by a tall, bearded man whose unkempt hair and clothes told the story of someone down on their luck. Willie resigned himself to the discomfort and settled back to enjoy what he would later describe as the feeling of being brought back from the dead.

The big jet departed, making a climbing turn toward its destination. Soon the seat belt sign was switched off and an attractive flight attendant began working her way up the isle taking drink orders. Willie ordered Sierra Nevada Pale Ale and, seeing the hangdog look on the face of his obviously cash-strapped seatmate, generously asked if he would like a drink too.

"It's on me," said Willie. "Feeling pretty good today. Might say I just hit the jackpot."

The tall man adjusted his sunglasses, thought for a moment, then in a soft, grateful voice replied, "Thanks. I think I will."

"What can I bring you?" asked the flight attendant.

"Live it up," coaxed Willie.

"That's very kind of you," said the man. He spoke to the attendant without taking his eyes off his new friend. "Glenlivet . . . on the rocks."

The End

Printed in the United States
135771LV00001B/1/P

9 781432 727352